Slip

Low Blow #2

Charity Parkerson

--Warning: This book is intended for readers over the age of 18.

Copyright © 2016 Charity Parkerson

Editor: Hercules Editing and Consultants

Photographer: RLS Images/ Randy Sewell

Cover Model: Jason Estes

ISBN-10:1-946099-07-4

ISBN-13:978-1-946099-07-5

Introduction

Kaz knows Boston isn't a good person. He just doesn't care.

Boston's looks alone could only be the work of the devil. His wicked smile, sexual expertise, and black heart are further proof the man had to have been created by Lucifer himself. He's tried ruining Kaz's best friend's life and has never been faithful to a soul. None of it matters. Kaz still can't stay away. He tells himself Boston means nothing. Kaz can quit him any time he likes. As long as Boston remains a secret, no one gets hurt... Right?

As the former cruiserweight champion, Boston is used to having the world at his feet. There have been few things in his life that have made him feel an ounce of guilt. Kaz is no different. Boston saw him, wanted him, and then set out to have him. He knows Kaz thinks to keep him a secret. But Boston hasn't gotten this far in life by hiding in the shadows.

When their relationship takes an unexpected turn and is shoved into the light, Kaz finds himself at a crossroad. He can accept the life he's always known, saving his heart and oldest friendship, or risk everything on the bad boy who can give him the world.

Chapter 1

Slip: A basic defense strategy used to avoid taking a hit.

Kaz didn't think receptions in general had been devised by the devil. However, this one was certainly taking place in Hell. The music was too loud. People stood too close. He hated everyone from the bottom of his heart. His ex had gotten married earlier in the day. It was a match made in heaven. Kaz was fucking miserable. He was happy for Liam. Really, he was, but he hurt for himself. In the back of his mind, Kaz had always secretly believed they'd get back together someday. When Liam had started dating his downstairs neighbor, Gunnar, Kaz knew he'd lost his chance. Kaz loved Liam enough to put on a smile for him, but he still hurt all the way to his soul.

Drink in hand, his third to be exact, Kaz searched for an open table. He didn't want to dance, nor did he have any desire to stand on the edge of the dancefloor, looking like an idiot. Nope. Kaz wanted to sit with his Jack and Coke and pretend to be fine while drinking himself into oblivion. He'd already ducked Liam's sister, Bree, twice, when she tried pulling him out on the dancefloor. Fuck that. He might have to fake it, but he didn't have to go that far. Spotting a familiar ginger that once made his mouth water, Kaz made a beeline and snagged the empty seat next to Aden, Gunnar's trainer. The man was built like a mountain. Kaz had never thought he'd care for a man like that. It was way out of his type, but he'd been out of his type-zone for a while now.

"You never stopped by Merge for that whiskey," Kaz said as he filled the seat next to Aden. The last time Kaz had seen Aden, he'd interrupted Aden's training session with Gunnar. Kaz had promised Aden a drink if he'd stop by Merge, as way of apology. Aden's green gaze slid Kaz's way. The man had some real sexiness going for him. Mostly, it was the eyes and his size. The man was built in all the perfect places.

"Aye, about that." Damn. The thick Irish accent was another of Aden's better traits. Kaz had forgotten that part. "I don't like clubs."

Kaz couldn't argue with him there. Merge had been Kaz's home since he'd turned twenty-one. At the time, he'd been young and stupid. He'd thought working as a bouncer would get him all the ass. In truth, he'd been right. Then, one day, he'd gotten used to the hours. Working three nights a week for ten hours a night while getting paid for working forty was hard to beat. Now, the place felt closer to being a prison.

"Honestly, I've been thinking about finding a new job. Hanging out in a club, even though I'm getting paid, is starting to feel ridiculous at my age."

"It's nothing to do with age," Aden said, his voice thick with laughter. "It's the people. I can't stand all the damn hair gel."

Aden's claim pulled a surprise bark of laughter from Kaz, but Aden wasn't finished.

"Oh, and the feckin' skinny jeans. Everyone there looks like a giant poodle shaved up and hair sprayed out for the dog show. Have you ever tried seducing someone wearing skinny jeans?"

Kaz shook his head, laughing too hard to speak.

"It's bloody awful. If I'm oiling up someone's ankles, it had best be because we're about to try some freaky shit. Not because their jeans are stuck."

Clearing his throat, Kaz tried getting his laughter under control. He swiped at his eyes. "Are you saying you'd rather take home a man who's sagging?"

Aden shook his head. "Even though that's a sight

better than moose knuckles, I'll pass on that as well. Give me a man in regular trousers, please."

Kaz looked at his suit, something he never wore, but did so for Liam. "I'd say mine are little fancy at the moment, but they fit like they're supposed to, so... Can I buy you that drink?"

The humor left Aden's eyes. "About that, I also don't care to mess with Boston's leavings."

It was a punch to the throat. Kaz couldn't deny Aden's claim. He also couldn't figure out how Aden had known. No one knew. At least, Kaz had thought no one knew. He'd been so careful. Since Boston was Gunnar's ex, and he'd tried ruining Gunnar's relationship with Liam, Kaz had been determined no one would ever know. Aden did. Kaz was speechless and oddly hurt. The entire day had been something out of a nightmare for him. He'd watched the man who'd once been the love of his life marry someone else. For a few minutes, he'd laughed again, thanks to Aden. But, once again, Kaz was back to being himself—the one who wasn't good enough for anyone.

He stood. While keeping his expression carefully blank, Kaz pushed his chair back in. "Thanks for the chat. It was nice seeing you again."

A flash of regret passed over Aden's features. It was

lost on Kaz. They didn't know each other. Not really. Aden was obviously a man used to saying what he thought. It didn't matter at all, except it did.

"I meant no offense."

Kaz motioned for Aden to stop. "It's fine. Enjoy your night."

Aden started to say more. Kaz walked away without listening. He couldn't hear another word. The day Boston had shown up at his door, intent on apologizing to Liam, but ending up in Kaz's bed, it had saved Kaz's life. For hundreds of reasons, everything they'd done had been wrong. Most of those reasons had to do with Liam. He'd known he'd regret Boston. Kaz hadn't realized it would come back to haunt him tonight, and that when it did, it would have nothing to do with Liam.

"Gunnar and Liam don't know," Aden called at his back, sounding as if it was some attempt to undo his sucker punch.

Turning, Kaz continued away. Walking backward, he spread his arms wide and let the world see his heart. "Doesn't matter. I've already lost everything."

Without wasting another minute on someone who thought him below the dirt on his shoes, Kaz walked away. Looked like he'd be going back to his job in hell after all. No sense in trying to better himself. Maybe he should send Aden some flowers or something. He owed the man a huge thank you for reminding Kaz of his place: beneath everyone.

*

After driving home on autopilot, Kaz stopped inside his house only long enough to toss his jacket on the couch before heading out the back door. Damn, he hated wearing a suit. He should change but couldn't find the energy. The heat of the day still lingered on the air, bringing a fine sheen of sweat to Kaz's skin. He loved his small place right on the water. The ocean could fix a lot. Unfortunately, tonight, nothing felt right. His skin felt all wrong—like it belonged to someone else.

Aden's words kept floating through Kaz's mind. He hadn't thought anyone knew about Boston. It didn't matter. Would Liam hate him? Another fucking mark against him with Liam. It was like he couldn't stop failing the man he once loved more than life, even with who he'd chosen to be with next.

"I like this place better than your old apartment. You can open your back door and step into the ocean. Home ownership suits you."

Kaz jumped as Boston appeared from the darkness. He tried not to show the man his surprise. "What are you doing here?"

"Key Largo is growing on me," Boston said, making Kaz wonder if he purposely misunderstood the question. "My whole life, I'd expected this place to be touristy, but it's not. It's just a small town. I love how quiet it is. Hell, there isn't even a Wal-Mart," Boston added as he slipped in behind Kaz and wrapped his arms around him. "New Orleans is crowded and loud. Plus, you're not there."

The worst part of Boston's touch was that Kaz didn't want to push him away. *You don't know Boston. He takes and drains, making you want it while hating him for it.* Gunnar's words ran through Kaz's mind, as they had a thousand times since starting this thing with Boston. Boston was Gunnar's ex. He'd know the man better than anyone. The citrusy scent of Boston's cologne engulfed Kaz along with the man's warmth. His supple lips caressed Kaz's nape. Chill bumps rose on Kaz's skin.

Boston's fingers worked on the buttons of Kaz's shirt. "What's with the get-up? Did I miss tonight's prom?"

Since Boston asked the questions against Kaz's neck, his lips brushing Kaz's skin with every syllable, Kaz couldn't think of a cutting retort to match Boston's smartass tone. "I was at a wedding."

Boston's fingers froze. His tone changed, going flat. "Liam's?"

Kaz nodded, doing his best to push the ache from his heart. "I was his groomsman. His sister, Bree, beat me out for best man, but I'm not insulted." A low chuckle escaped him. "In spite of how small she is, she probably can out man me in every way. She could definitely out drink and cuss me. Hell, she could probably beat me in arm wrestling, because she cheats." The humor drained Kaz. That was supposed to be his sister-in-law. Life. It was cruel.

The tugging on his shirt resumed as Boston slid a few more buttons loose. "Let me guess. Aden stood up for Gunnar. Along with... Huh. I'm stumped."

"Some guy from Phoenix. Troy," Kaz supplied.

Cool air brushed Kaz's chest as his shirt fell open. Boston flattened his palms against Kaz's stomach, massaging his skin. To his shame, Kaz's body responded as if Boston held his dick.

"I don't know him," Boston said as he dragged Kaz's shirt down his shoulders. "What else did I miss?"

Since Boston didn't sound as if he truly cared and was only keeping Kaz distracted while he stole Kaz's clothes, Kaz wanted to rattle him. "You're lucky I was here when you showed up. I thought about seducing

13

Aden."

A low rumble of laughter caressed Kaz's throat along with Boston's lips. "Luck had nothing to do with it, and you should have. Two lovers are always better than one."

A hint of anger ignited in Kaz's gut. "Two of anything is always better than one."

"That's not true," Boston said, sliding his hands toward Kaz's waistband. "There're plenty of things I don't want in pairs. Speeding tickets, black eyes... flat tires."

At Boston's intentional pause, Kaz's eyes fell closed and regret washed over him. It seemed everyone knew all of his darkest secrets. His chin dropped to his chest and Kaz stared at Boston's hands as they tugged at his clothing.

"Are you planning to invite me in, Kaz? Or would you rather your neighbors watch us from their windows? I'm not opposed to that, but it's up to you."

Kaz didn't budge. His knees wouldn't work. "How did you know about the tires?" Even to his ears, Kaz sounded deadly.

"I saw you. Liam's car was parked two spaces over from me. I was sitting in my rental, plotting my next move."

Bile rose in Kaz's throat. That made it official. Boston had seen him slash Liam's tires. It had been the act of a desperate man, pulling the last card he had. He'd known Liam would turn to him. They'd have one more night alone. Kaz knew he was a sad person, but Boston, he'd seen it all. "Yet you let it happen."

Boston shrugged. Kaz felt it more than saw it. "At the time, I had no idea who you were or why you'd slash such a nice person's tires, but I knew I could use it to my advantage." Boston opened his mouth over the cords of Kaz's neck, bringing chill bumps to Kaz's skin before continuing. "So when Liam left work that night, I followed him outside and offered him a ride. When he didn't accept, some strange sort of chivalry rose in my chest." A humorless laugh filled the space between them. From anyone else, it would've been ugly. Boston made it sound sexy. "As I said, I didn't know you. I worried you might hurt him. So I refused to let Liam make the walk to Merge alone. It's almost funny now that I know you," Boston said, cutting Kaz to the bone. "On the way to Merge, Liam mentioned his ex working there, and all the pieces clicked. By the time we made it to the club, I was outraged on his behalf—angry Gunnar wasn't there to protect him. Enraged he'd turn to you—the man responsible for his predicament. I was

15

genuinely pissed off he was surrounded by people who would treat him so poorly. Me. The person plotting to ruin him. I'm not a nice person, Kaz."

The words fell from Boston's lips, sounding like the deepest confession. Boston's hand dipped inside Kaz's waistband, palming his erection. "But I don't think you want a nice guy. Not anymore," Boston added, proving he really did know all of Kaz's dirty secrets. With Boston touching him, Kaz couldn't work up a care over what Boston knew. Maybe it was for the best because there was one aspect Boston hadn't pointed out—Kaz wasn't a good person either.

*

Kaz rocked against Boston's palm the same shameless way he always did. As if Boston hadn't confessed anything. Boston kept his touch light, purposely torturing him. A faint hint of cologne still lingered at Kaz's throat. Boston went looking for more. With his face buried in the crook of Kaz's neck, Boston inhaled. A low moan escaped the man in his arms. Satisfaction roared through Boston.

"Were you planning to invite me in? Or are we staying out here?" Boston asked. While keeping a tight hold on Kaz's pants so they wouldn't slide to the ground, Boston dragged the material down one hip,

16

pressing his point. "It's your choice."

"Inside." Kaz's answer was low and breathless. It made Boston's dick twitch.

Before Boston could urge Kaz toward the door, Kaz spun in his hold. Their mouths collided. The memory of the first time they'd kissed slammed into Boston. He hadn't seen it coming then either. In a moment of desperate loneliness, he'd propositioned Kaz. Boston had expected Kaz to shut him down with a huge dose of scorn. Instead, Kaz had shot to his feet and captured Boston's lips with his. His shock had quickly been washed away by lust. Kaz's kiss was part skill and all perfection. He kissed like most men hoped to get their dicks sucked—hard and deep. Boston massaged Kaz's waist as he encircled it. A chuckle rose in his throat as he tried shoving his hands down the back of Kaz's pants only to find Kaz had too tight of a hold on them to allow any give. Kaz smiled against Boston's lips as Boston's laugh vibrated through their kiss.

"No way are my neighbors seeing my ass tonight," Kaz said before going in deep for another kiss. He walked Boston backward toward the door. Ragged breathing filled the night air when Kaz pulled away long enough to reach past Boston and open the door. Their gazes collided and held. "I know I shouldn't give

17

you the satisfaction, but I missed you."

As with all things Kaz, Boston was equally blown away and disappointed. In his life, he'd never felt more desired and unwanted at the same time as he did with Kaz. None of it mattered. No matter how either of them felt, soon Kaz would bury himself in Boston's body, and Boston would still be the winner.

"Two weeks," Kaz said as he kicked the door closed behind them. "In the past six months, you've never stayed away that long. I didn't think you were coming back."

Boston pulled his shirt over his head to give himself a minute. Instant rage hit his bloodstream at Kaz's words. Not coming back? Seriously? "It was thirteen days. Not two weeks," Boston said, tossing his shirt aside. He tried capturing Kaz's lips once more, but Kaz leaned back out of his reach.

"You've been counting the days?"

In a deep-seated need to protect himself, Boston pushed Kaz's hand aside, forcing him to let go of his pants. They slid to the floor. Boston's gaze dropped, taking in the gorgeous picture Kaz presented. "I passed first grade," Boston said, hearing the lust in his voice. "I know how to add. Goddamn, Kaz," he added, forgetting the topic. Kaz's body was tight and huge. He

18

had a natural dark-skinned hue, making anyone who spent time in the sun jealous. But Boston's gaze was locked on the wet spot forming on Kaz's underwear, where the man's dick leaked in anticipation. It was a completely undervalued trait—rampant lust. Being wanted, the way Kaz always responded to Boston; it was compelling. There was no way Boston could stop coming back for more. His brain finally went full-circle, finding their topic once more.

Lifting his gaze, Boston met Kaz's intense jade stare. "Yes. I've been counting the days."

At his admission, Kaz sprang. He closed the distance between them, attacking Boston's mouth. Boston's lips stung and his body burned. Kaz was ruthless as he tore at the remainder of their clothing. Everywhere Kaz touched roared with need. His tight grip threatened to ruin Boston for all others. Boston feared that might already be the case. Slipping a foot through Boston's, Kaz pulled a takedown move. It shouldn't have shocked Boston. No doubt Kaz was used to pulling every dirty fight trick in the book at work when having to diffuse a situation. But the strength Kaz showed, easing Boston to the floor; that not only surprised Boston, it also sent his lust through the roof.

"Tell me you have a condom on you," Kaz demanded on a growl. He snagged Boston's jeans and dragged them closer.

"In my wallet."

The way Kaz tore through the contents of Boston's wallet with shaking hands had Boston panting. He was near to writhing on the floor beneath Kaz. His dick screamed for attention. He thought he'd tear his skin off if Kaz didn't get inside him. By the time Kaz suited up, Boston might've begged. Words left his mouth. Even to his ears, they made no sense.

"Boston."

Boston's gaze shot to Kaz's. Those jade eyes. Boston stopped breathing.

"Moan for me," Kaz demanded as he finally gave Boston what he needed and eased inside him.

Kaz need not have asked. Boston couldn't have contained his pleasure if he'd wanted. With his head thrown back, Boston gasped for air. Sounds he couldn't control ripped from his throat as Kaz's dick stretched him wide. Kaz had a way of tilting at an angle and grinding down on Boston that made the world disappear. There wasn't a single thought in his head. His mind was narrowed to a pinpoint. The only thing that mattered to him was what Kaz did to his body.

Without warning, an orgasm roared through Boston. Like that, with no stroking of his cock whatsoever. That was what Kaz did for him. Something no one else ever had. This relationship—whatever it was—was a sickness.

"Damn, Kaz. Holy shit," Boston breathed, trying to catch his breath as the ecstasy rolled on and cum coated Boston's stomach and chest.

Kaz captured Boston's lips, biting before going deep. His kiss was animalistic, as if they were fighting for dominance. A rhythmic noise left the back of Kaz's throat as he came, making Boston feel consumed.

Ragged breaths, matching the way Kaz's shoulders heaved, fell from Kaz's lips as he kissed a path from Boston's mouth to his ear. "Thirteen days is too long. Don't pull that shit again."

Boston nodded, incapable of speech. He'd had his reasons for staying away so long. Kaz had missed him. It wouldn't happen again.

Chapter 2

There was nothing except a note on the pillow, proving Boston had been there. Kaz tried pretending it wasn't disappointment filling his chest. After unfolding the single sheet of paper, Kaz read the three words inside— *I'll be back.* That was it. With Boston, that could've meant in thirty minutes or days. Kaz wanted to tear the paper to shreds and scream at the top of his lungs. In the end, he did neither. Instead, he did the same as always. He got up and dressed, pretending as if nothing happened. It was another day with the same old losses.

A knock on the door pulled Kaz from his growing depression. He was always this way when Boston disappeared. Hope rose in his chest as he headed for the door. It died as quickly as it took life. Boston wasn't much on knocking. A quick peek through the peephole confirmed his thoughts but doubled his curiosity. Kaz tried rearranging his features into some semblance of welcome as he opened the door.

"Aden. This is..."

A deep line appeared in Aden's cheek as his mouth lifted in one corner. "I got your address from Liam.

Hope you don't mind. Figured if I got your number, you'd either refuse to answer or would hang up once you knew it was me."

He might have, so Kaz couldn't deny it.

"Anyhow," Aden said when Kaz held his silence. "I'm thinking I owe you an apology. Since I don't do it often, as I'm not much on regretting things I say, I hoped I could take you to lunch as a way of making things up to you." Aden shifted from one foot to the other, looking uncomfortable. His effort meant more than any words could.

"Did you have someplace in mind?"

Aden's expression brightened when he realized Kaz wouldn't shut him down. He nodded. "I was thinking that place owned by the old football coach. It's peaceful."

He knew the place. They had a deck out on the water. It was peaceful. "Let me get some shoes on, and we'll go." The relief written on Aden's face made Kaz's discomfort worthwhile. It wasn't like he hadn't said things he wished he could take back, and it wasn't often anyone apologized to Kaz. He'd take any olive branch he could get at this point.

Kaz wasn't good at small talk, but they somehow made it through their meal.

It took Aden that long to break. "Forgive me the curiosity, but where are you from?"

Kaz bit back a chuckle at the question. Everyone always had the same one.

"I've been chewing on it since we first met, but damned if I can figure it out. You use an Englishman's tongue, but your golden skin color makes me think you crossed a different pond to get here."

With a shake of his head, Kaz let Aden know he wasn't offended by the inquiry. "Everyone always has the same trouble. That's because I'm an odd duck. My mum was English and my father was Korean. I can speak both fluently." Kaz laughed at his joke. As usual, he was the only one who thought it was funny. He cleared his throat. "Anyhow, while my parents were on holiday in Miami, I decided to make an appearance four weeks ahead of schedule, so I have a dual citizenship." He hadn't been lying about being odd. There was more. Kaz braced himself for Aden's mockery. "Then, when I was fifteen, my Korean father and English-born mum decided to fulfill their lifelong dream to open a real Italian pizza shop in Miami."

Instead of laughing, Aden cocked his head, as if attempting to work through Kaz's explanation. "That doesn't explain how you landed here in the Keys."

"Oh," Kaz said, recognizing he'd forgotten the most important part of his life story. "That was Liam. We worked at neighboring clubs in Miami, and sometimes, when he got off work, he'd make his way over to mine." Kaz shook his head at the memory. A smile touched his lips. "Of course, I didn't know he was coming from there. I wondered why he always showed up right before closing and too late to drink. When I found out he was taking his clothes off two doors down, I..." Kaz snapped his teeth together in horror. He couldn't believe he was having lunch with one man and speaking of another. Aden didn't appear offended, but Kaz was still mortified. "Apologies. I got sidetracked. As to your question, he lived here, so I had no issue with moving here with him where he could stay close to his family."

"What of your family?"

"They're still happily running the shop in Miami."

Aden shook his head. "Actually, I meant why haven't you moved back to be closer to your family since Liam is no longer keeping you here?"

Kaz shrugged. "I did for a while. What about you?" he asked, dodging any explanation. "How did an Irishman end up here?"

"Gunnar," Aden said, as if that was the whole story.

25

"Ah, okay."

Aden snorted. "I gather you've never seen Gunnar fight."

Kaz shook his head. "Only when he won the title, but I don't follow the sport, so he looked as I imagine a fighter would."

"Well, that's strange. But, me being me, it only took once, and that was back when he was no one." Aden set his elbows on the table and leaned closer. His eyes were bright with enthusiasm for the topic. Kaz was still trying to work out why Aden thought his answer strange. "I used to throw a punch or two in my younger days." Kaz eyed Aden's features at the comment. He had some laugh lines around his eyes, but honestly, he could've been thirty or fifty for all Kaz could tell. "But I'm a trainer at heart. Love polishing diamonds. Gunnar, he's the best of them all. I spotted it straight away. Even if he beefed up a few pounds and went for heavyweight, he'd shoot straight to the top with no stumbling in between. He could take the world."

"Why doesn't he?" Kaz asked, sucked into the story.

"Doesn't want it, does he? Gunnar's done the bright lights and travel. He's seen the underbelly. Having the world looking at you, willing to give you anything for a few blows to the head; it's a sickness. Poisons the blood. That's what happened to your fella, Boston. Twisted by too much fame."

"He's not my fellow," Kaz said without thought. He couldn't imagine Boston's reaction over being called that. Once the thought snuck in, Kaz was hooked. An image of Boston, head thrown back and cords straining as he came, filled Kaz's head. He shifted in his seat to ease his body's swift reaction. If anyone was twisted, it was Kaz.

"That's not the way I heard it," Aden said, jerking Kaz back to reality.

His mouth went dry. "What?"

Aden nodded. "In my business, you hear all manner of shit, from sponsorship spats to gossip about people's affairs. It's hard to hide his constant trips this way, and being as how he ain't coming to see Gunnar, people were curious. Those in the know say he's claiming it's you he's set on nowadays."

That sounded oddly ominous. Kaz fiddled with his napkin on the table before realizing his nervous motions said too much. He dropped his hands to his lap.

Aden laughed. "You might want to stop worrying at your bottom lip if you're trying not to give yourself away. I can't imagine anyone would turn down Boston, given half the chance. Touched by Lucifer, he was. No one looks like him and charms like him without the Devil's consent."

Kaz wiped his palms on his jeans. He still had nothing.

Aden wasn't finished. "Thing is, it's a mask. Underneath is a rotted soul."

"That's not true," Kaz said, wanting to bite off his tongue but refusing to take it back. As the words left his lips, Kaz realized how much he meant them. "I get that he cheated on Gunnar. He was wrong for that. But hell, if I start judging everyone by their past, what hope is there left for me?"

For a full minute, Aden eyed Kaz in silence. "You're already wrapped up with a bow. I'm sorry to see that. You'll get hurt."

Kaz felt his jaw tick. "It won't be the first time."

"Aye. I'm sure of it."

"Thank you for lunch."

Aden continued to hold Kaz's gaze as if Kaz hadn't signaled an end to this mess. "I hope it isn't the last."

Before he could stop it from happening, Kaz scoffed. "Why? I'm obviously a joke to you."

A small smile touched Aden's lips. "Not at all. I see

you the same as Boston, I suppose."

Kaz snorted. "No one sees me at all."

"You're wrong," Aden said, pushing his chair away from the table. "People see you too clearly. That's why you're easy prey."

The ride home was made in silence. When they reached Kaz's tiny slice of heaven, Aden spotted Boston first, making the situation more awkward. "I'm guessing you'd like to retract your statement about him not being your fella."

Kaz eyed the unfamiliar car parked in his driveway. Most likely a rental. His gaze shot toward the house. Kaz's heart rate betrayed him. Boston looked damn delicious, kicked back in the rocker on Kaz's front porch with his feet balanced on the railing.

"Or you could say nothing at all," Aden added as they climbed from the car.

He couldn't. The way Boston's blue gaze followed Kaz's every move, as if waiting for the moment he could pounce, had Kaz's blood singing.

"I didn't know he'd be here," Kaz said under his breath too late for it to count.

"Aden," Boston said. His gaze never left Kaz's.

"Boston," Aden said, acknowledging Boston's greeting with humor filling his voice.

Boston ignored him. "I left you a note."

"Right chummy of you, but I don't suppose you meant me," Aden said, his laughter deepening.

Boston's gaze slid Aden's way. Without a word, he went back to watching Kaz.

"I saw," Kaz said, unsure of what to do. Not only did Boston not look angry, Kaz knew in his gut that Boston didn't care about him enough to work up an ounce of jealousy.

Boston dropped his feet to the ground and sat forward. "I said I'd be back."

Kaz nodded. "I read that."

Aden cleared his throat, reminding Kaz of his presence. "Being as how you've got more men than you can handle, I think I'll head out."

Tearing his gaze away from Boston, he focused on Aden. "Thanks again for lunch." He didn't know what else to say. Anytime Boston said he'd be back, it could mean anything from a few minutes to weeks. This wasn't him. He didn't cheat. If this was cheating. Fuck. Kaz hated this.

Aden must've seen the desperation in Kaz's eyes. A sexy smile touched Aden's lips. "Now you owe me a drink and lunch. You know where to find me when this comes to its inevitable end." Switching his attention

30

Boston's way, Aden dipped his chin at Boston. "Blessedly short, as always."

Kaz looked back and forth between them with no clue how to react. The wicked smile twisting Boston's lips matched the glint in his eyes.

"I'm sure we'll see each other again soon," Boston said without ever looking away from Kaz. There were times, like now, when Boston made Kaz want to beat his head against the wall. He would've paid any amount of money to see inside Boston's head. Boston was impossible to read. Kaz was one hundred percent positive he meant nothing at all to Boston. Yet the man kept showing up. And the things Boston did to Kaz's body, wow. As sure as Kaz was that Boston didn't care about him was how positive Kaz was he'd beg Boston for more. There was an emptiness in being with Boston. Aden's words at lunch hit home. It was a twisted thing, wanting Boston.

"I took a little trip to Miami," Boston offered the moment they were alone, thankfully not forcing Kaz to ask where he'd gone. "There's an amazing little pizza place there."

Kaz's heart dropped.

"Your mom says you never called her back the other day. I told her I would remind you, so call your mom."

Yes. It was every bit as bad as Kaz feared. "I'll get around to it."

Boston ignored Kaz's claim. "She was very helpful, putting me in touch with your boss, Jeff. Nice guy. No wonder you've stayed at Merge for ten years. He seems easy to work with."

Kaz didn't know if he should laugh or throw a punch. Instead, he held on, waiting to see how bad this would get. He didn't have to wait long.

"Jeff tells me, unlike the rest of his employees, you never miss work. He was glad you took this weekend off and was more than happy to give you next weekend off as well. After I autographed a few items for the bar, that is."

"Is that so?" Kaz had no idea why he sounded so unconcerned, but there it was.

Boston nodded. "Now you're free to stay with me in New Orleans for the next week and a half. Oh, and I've already let your parents know where they can reach us so they won't worry."

The desire to rage, laugh, and cheer duked it out inside Kaz's head, leaving him unsure where he'd land. "Did you pack my bags too while I was gone?"

A regretful sounding sigh fell from Boston's

gorgeous lips. "The door was locked."

"I'm surprised you let that stop you," Kaz said as he moved to unlock the door.

"We don't have time to wait to get a busted door fixed," Boston said, obviously unashamed. "Our flight leaves in four hours."

Kaz stumbled as he crossed the threshold at Boston's words. The tickets were bought. He didn't know why anything surprised him when it came to Boston. "What if I refuse?"

"Then you won't be able to get the ten boxes of beignet mix I told your mom you'd pick up."

"I'm willing to bet I could order that online," Kaz shot back without missing a beat.

Boston shut the door behind them. "You can't order a week and a half alone with me online."

"I'm not so sure that's true."

Boston's features snapped closed. In the best well-played use of silence in history, Boston said nothing. Kaz felt like shit. All the way to his core.

"If I've got four hours, I'd better pack quick. It'll take us almost two just to get to the airport."

Boston nodded. If he was happy about Kaz giving in, he didn't show it. "There's no telling what security looks like and I need to drop off my rental."

His voice had gone dead in a way that twisted Kaz's insides. Why did he do these things? Boston was nothing but good to him, and Kaz always punished him for it. Why? Did he want to hurt him for being high handed or keep him in his place? Maybe he did it for all the reasons Aden stated at lunch. It didn't matter why. Kaz was wrong.

Instead of heading for the bedroom to pack, Kaz closed the distance between them. He fought the urge to attack Boston's mouth the way he always did. This time, he moved slow, barely brushing his lips against Boston's until Boston opened for him. Even then, their lips clung, as they shared the same air, until Kaz dipped inside, searching for Boston's tongue. When he found it, they lightly stroked before twining together. It was sweet. It was unlike any kiss they'd ever shared. Kaz's chest tightened.

His hands found Boston's cheeks. He gently held Boston's face between his hands. Boston's hands landed on Kaz's hips. Neither of them forced the other any closer. Kaz took Boston's bottom lip between his and held it there, savoring the moment. As he pulled away, Kaz caught a glimpse of heaven. Blue eyes made brighter by the flush on Boston's cheeks. This man was arresting, and he was here with Kaz, demanding more of Kaz's time. Kaz was the king of regretting his words. That didn't mean he couldn't try taking them back.

"I'm sorry. There's nothing I'd rather do than spend the next week and a half with you. Come help me figure out what to pack. I've never been to New Orleans."

Boston's hold tightened on Kaz's hips. "Kaz, I..."

Kaz held his breath and waited.

A flash of something unnamed passed over Boston's features before disappearing. An odd sense of loss filled Kaz. He felt like he'd missed out on hearing something wonderful.

"If you're missing anything important when we get there, I'll buy it for you. Otherwise, the weather there matches here."

Rather than shake the thoughts from Boston's head as he wanted to do, Kaz turned away. He needed to get his things together. Then he could spend his days trying to figure Boston out.

Chapter 3

There was something cold and empty about Boston's house. Kaz couldn't put his finger on it. It was clean, almost as if no one lived there. As far as Kaz could tell, there wasn't a speck of dust on anything. No clutter or pictures of family on the walls. It was unnerving.

"Do you want to put your things away?"

Kaz shifted from foot to foot at Boston's question. "I'm not sure. My suitcase might ruin the OCDish perfection of your living area."

A low rumble of laugher filled the air as Boston snagged Kaz's suitcase and headed for an open doorway on the right. "I haven't been here since the last time the cleaning company came through. They're efficient."

Even though Boston's claim eased Kaz's worries by a hair, there was still something gnawing at the back of his mind. He just expected Boston's place to be different. The man was a world champion boxer. There should've been some hint of pride in something in his life. If his home was any reflection of the man... "How long have you lived here?" Kaz asked, following on Boston's heels into what had to be the man's bedroom.

Its dark colors matched the man's personality, and it smelled like Boston's cologne.

"Since I won my first title, so ten years, I guess."

Ten years. "You don't have any pictures of your family on the walls." Kaz couldn't let it go.

"Seems vain to hang pictures of myself on the wall. I have a mirror," Boston said as he set Kaz's suitcase on the floor inside the bedroom.

Kaz was still trying to work out Boston's words when Boston turned and snagged Kaz around the waist. In a move almost too quick to follow, Kaz hit the mattress. With a huge grin stretching his lips, Boston slowly followed him down. He straddled Kaz's hips and held his gaze. The breath caught at the back of Kaz's throat. Every day, it got a little harder to hate himself for wanting to be with this man. Aden was right; Kaz would get hurt.

"I never thought I'd talk you into coming here."

"You didn't," Kaz said, pointing out the obvious. "There was much highhandedness involved." Kaz smoothed his palms up Boston's thighs. "For all you know, I might've agreed if you'd simply asked."

Boston's expression turned serious. "Would you have come here if I'd asked?"

A flippant response about how they'd never know

raced to Kaz's tongue. The way Boston watched him, as if holding his breath, caused the words to die away. "Yes," Kaz said, knowing his admission gave Boston another ounce of power over him. "I would've leapt at the chance."

Boston's mouth lifting in one corner was all the indication the man gave that Kaz's answer affected him in any way. "You might change your mind when I tell you that I have to attend an event tonight."

"Have fun with that."

Kaz bit back a laugh at Boston's eye roll. "Nope. You're going with."

"An event sounds like something requiring fancy clothing. So, once again, have fun with that."

A sexy smile, hot enough to steal Kaz's breath, stretched Boston's lips. "I don't like to brag. Well, okay, I love to brag. I do it all the time. Love that shit. Anyhow, I'm worth a lot of money. Like a shit-ton of money. You don't have to worry over what you'll wear tonight. I've got you covered."

He didn't know whether to be enraged or laugh. As much as Kaz didn't want Boston spending money on him, he was smart enough to know he wasn't winning this argument. Boston was shady and underhanded. This man would do whatever it took to get his way. Kaz couldn't compete with his cunning.

"I'll pay for my own clothes. Thank you."

Boston's smile widened. Kaz realized too late that he'd been played. "It's adorable when you're angry with me. A line appears between your eyes," Boston said smoothing out the line with his thumb. "Your jaw hardens," he added as he leaned down and kissed Kaz's jaw. He didn't move away. Boston's breath fanned across Kaz's throat. "I don't want to go alone tonight."

Goddamn it. Boston always knew what to say and how to say it to make Kaz want to give him anything. It wasn't enough for the man to get his way. No. It was as if Boston had some strange need to twist Kaz to his will while making him like it. The saddest part was— Kaz craved the sensation of being bent to suit Boston. A dark, sick, perverse longing lived in Kaz's gut. He wanted to lie at Boston's feet and give him more.

As Kaz's palms flattened against the bare skin of Boston's back, he realized he'd been blindly searching for a way to get closer. "I wouldn't let you be alone."

Even Kaz could read between the lines in his tone. He meant "ever." Kaz knew all too well what it was like to have no one—to be alone in a crowd. For every ounce of weakness Boston showed, Kaz sank deeper into something unnamed. Sometimes, he was scared shitless he'd drown and never notice until it was too late. This man could hurt him. Maybe worse than he'd ever been hurt before.

*

After much fighting and thirty minutes of Kaz not speaking to him, Boston convinced Kaz to let him buy the man a tux. Damn, was Boston glad for it. Kaz looked sexy as sin all decked out. Boston seriously considered cancelling their plans for the night at the first sight of him. Unfortunately, as one of the guests of honor, Boston had no choice. They had to go. Three hours in, with one meal consumed and an award tucked under his arm for donating a massive amount of money to charity, exhaustion hit full force. Not that Boston intended to allow anyone the satisfaction of seeing it. He'd learned long ago, the more people who cheered for him, the more people who couldn't wait to see him fail in some way.

Boston hated these events. He didn't mind giving money to worthy causes but couldn't stand the pretentious dinners thrown in money's honor. The air was too thick. There were too many people. He was tired of everyone looking at him and wanting to talk to him. Kaz appeared every bit as miserable. Anyone else who looked at Kaz probably thought the man was fine. Boston could tell different. Kaz was bored off his ass. Boston fucking despised that. When he'd invited Kaz to stay, he'd known he was maneuvering Kaz into coming with him tonight, but the last thing Boston wanted was for Kaz to lament his time there. Boston eased toward the door, hoping to make an escape the first chance he had.

A small group of people blocked the exit, making Boston want to groan. One of the men was a tall, blond journalist who always managed to snag a few words with Boston before Boston could get away. Seemed tonight would be no different. By the glint in the man's brown eyes, he knew Boston had hoped to disappear without notice. Boston intentionally turned his back on the man and gave his attention to a dark-haired man who Boston couldn't put a name to. It was Cal or Mal. Hell, it may've been just Al. The man's mouth moved, but Boston paid him no mind, instead choosing to focus on Kaz's conversation with the reporter.

"I don't believe we've met. I'm Daniel Long with *The Daily Sports Review.*"

"Kaz," Kaz said, accepting Daniel's outstretched hand.

Boston kept one ear locked on the pair, attempting

to hear their every word while also focusing on the man talking to him about some upcoming event for the homeless, or maybe he'd said buying sports equipment for schools. Hell, Boston didn't know. He was too focused on Kaz and Daniel. It wasn't that Boston didn't like Daniel. In truth, he didn't feel one way or the other about the man. Like everyone else in the room, the journalist served a purpose. Anything Daniel chose to print about Boston could either enhance or ruin Boston's reputation. Boston couldn't care less either way. He'd already done everything in life he'd set out to accomplish. But it was Daniel's job to fluster people—get them to reveal too much. Boston hadn't coerced Kaz into coming to this event with the intention of exposing him to scorn. Kaz belonged to him. Boston wouldn't let anything happen to him. He was right to worry.

"What do you do for a living, Kaz?"

"I work security for a club in Miami." The problem wasn't what Kaz did for a living. It was how he told people what he did for a living. Boston had always believed—no matter what job a person held—if they said it with pride, then no one could scoff. When Kaz told anyone where he worked, he always sounded ashamed. Tonight was no different. Daniel had his blood.

Boston rudely turned away from the dark-haired man who'd been speaking to him and focused on Daniel. The journalist's smirk told Boston everything he needed to know about the man's thoughts. Boston turned on the charm as he took Kaz's hand in his.

"Thank God Kaz has a steady job. One of us will need one."

Daniel's smirk fell away and his eyes sharpened. "So the rumors are true, then? You're retiring?"

Boston brought their clasped hands to his mouth and kissed the back of Kaz's before answering, "I didn't say that."

Daniel chuckled. "Actually, I'm certain you did. Have you promised an exclusive to someone else?"

"I never make promises to anyone, especially of exclusivity."

Once again, Daniel's smirk was firmly back in place. His gaze slid Kaz's way. Boston allowed his smile to turn wicked. He knew how to use his expressions to his advantage.

"Except to Kaz, of course," Boston added before Daniel had time to think of a smartass retort. His pause had been intentional. He wanted Daniel to believe Kaz would already know that without Boston having to say as much. Boston needed Daniel to think the comment had been for his benefit alone. A real couple wouldn't need to make such assurances. The sentiment would be understood.

Daniel's gaze turned calculating. "Can I quote you on that?"

Boston tried hiding his satisfaction. The man played right into his hands. "Of course. Would you like a photo to add to your story?" He'd been intentionally avoiding Kaz's gaze and his reaction, but at Boston's question, Kaz tried backing away. Boston held tight, refusing to let him escape.

Looking like a man who'd won the lotto, Daniel pulled out his cell phone. "I'll definitely take you up on that offer."

Boston glanced over. Kaz's jaw ticked, but he wasn't running. "Smile, babe. You're about to make some front page news." Kaz's gaze slid Boston's way. His sexy jade eyes softened when they landed on Boston. Boston's throat tightened at the telling reaction. Instead of moving in close and posing for Daniel's picture, Boston leaned in and brushed his lips against Kaz's. The world slipped away—the way it always did when they kissed. By the time Boston pulled back, Kaz's eyes were slightly unfocused and his lips parted on a pant. No one was sexier than Kaz in Boston's book. The man was important to Boston. That was why Boston couldn't let Kaz continue to pretend they were only friends.

"I'm sorry. Remind me of your last name, Kaz."

At Daniel's question, Kaz licked his lips, but he didn't look away from Boston as he answered, "Sobong."

"Thank you for the chat, Mr. Sobong. Boston, it's been a pleasure, as always," Daniel said, seemingly unbothered by the fact neither man paid him an ounce of attention.

"You too," Boston said, unsure if his answer made any sense. "Are you ready to get out of here?" he asked Kaz, hoping he wasn't alone in his need for privacy. "I'm freaking starving after that disaster of a meal."

Kaz chuckled. "I am too."

"Good. It's settled," Boston said, steering Kaz toward the door. "Let's hit the Burger Shack and make all the men jealous they didn't think of wearing their badass tuxes to get fast food."

"Sounds like the perfect date to me."

*

Sitting across from Boston in a fast food joint while wearing a three-thousand-dollar tuxedo, after having arrived in a '71 Hemi Cuda that probably went for two million at auction, was surreal as fuck. After twenty minutes in Boston's company, all those things disappeared. With his elbows braced on the table, Kaz listened to Boston tell a story about spending ten minutes looking for a pair of shoes he was wearing. He made sure he laughed in all the right places. In truth, he didn't absorb a word. Boston's constantly changing expressions kept Kaz fascinated.

Boston stopped talking and tilted his head to one side. His sexy smile had Kaz ready to shove aside the table between them to capture Boston's lips. "You didn't hear any of that, did you?"

"They were on your feet the whole time," Kaz dutifully repeated.

Boston's smile grew. The lines at the corners of his mouth deepened. "Actually, I've been talking about global warming for five minutes now."

Kaz's eyebrows snapped together. How the fuck had he zoned out that badly?

Boston laughed. It was hot as hell. The sound rumbled over Kaz's skin and tightened his groin. "Do I strike you as the type to discuss global warming?"

"You never can tell," Kaz said with a shrug. "Your mind is beautifully brilliant. It might take your mouth anywhere."

A wicked glint flashed in Boston's eyes. Kaz didn't miss it. "I want it noted I'm passing on an opportunity to make that into a sexual reference since we're in public."

"According to you, you don't mind a public display."

Without warning, Boston shot forward and captured Kaz's mouth. The kiss was a short one, but it still blew Kaz away.

"What were we talking about?"

At Kaz's question, Boston winked. "I was telling you I'm getting us a couple of milkshakes to go. Then I intend to take you home and make love to you for several hours."

Kaz blinked. "Okay." At Kaz's dazed response, Boston slipped from the booth to do as he promised.

*

"I think you have a problem."

Boston took a sip of his milkshake as he glanced over his shoulder at Kaz with both eyebrows raised in question.

Kaz laughed.

Boston fucking loved that sound.

"You're proving my point here."

Giving in, Boston bit. "What point is that?"

"That you have a problem. Is there a program for people who are addicted to milkshakes?"

He shrugged. "If there is, I want no part of it. I eat healthy ninety-eight percent of the time. Not to mention, I work my ass off at the gym. Everyone deserves one guilty pleasure." Boston locked the front door before snagging the back of Kaz's neck and pulling him in for a deep kiss. "Or two guilty pleasures," he said, releasing Kaz and going back to drinking his shake. "There's something I want to show you," he said, heading for the stairs without looking to see if Kaz would follow. He could feel Kaz at his back. Boston's skin tingled with awareness. "I realized on the way home that we didn't have time for a tour earlier. We were so busy trying to get ready for tonight, I didn't get to show you my favorite part of the house." He turned at the landing, going up a second set of stairs.

"Holy fuck, Boston. How many floors does this house have?"

Boston shrugged. "Only three."

"Only three," Kaz repeated under his breath.

His reaction pulled a chuckle from Boston. Really, his house wasn't ridiculous. He'd intentionally not spent every dime of his money on a home. It was just a place to rest his head. In his business, he did a lot of traveling. Plus, he'd never been certain New Orleans would stay his home. He could live anywhere.

"In my defense, the third floor is really only a room, leading to what I want to show you."

When they reached the top of the stairs, Boston could already see the blue water lit by pool lights, shimmering through the glass doors to his right. He didn't turn to check Kaz's reaction as he disengaged the alarm system leading to the pool. He'd been assured keeping this door separate from the rest of the system would keep any small children who might be visiting from going out the door unnoticed. He didn't know anyone with small children, but whatever. Better safe than sorry and all that.

"You have a pool. On the roof. There's a pool on your roof."

"It isn't very deep. Really only about to your waist, but I like it. Also, it's salt water, so it's easy to keep up."

"There's a pool on your roof," Kaz repeated. "Why do you have a pool on your roof?"

Boston set his shake aside and peeled off his jacket. "So I can do this without anyone watching," he said, untucking his shirt and pulling off his belt. With

Kaz's heated gaze watching Boston's every move as he removed each layer of clothing, Boston's dick leaked. By the time Boston was nude, a flush rode high on Kaz's cheeks and his bottom lip had color from him chewing on it.

Kaz's hands moved to the buttons on his jacket.

Boston reached out, stopping him. "I want to do it."

Kaz's eyes flashed with hunger as his hands fell away. Moving slowly, Boston slid each button loose on Kaz's jacket and shirt. He pulled the man's tie loose before shoving the open material down Kaz's shoulders, trapping his arms. With Kaz tangled in his jacket and shirt, Boston moved closer and touched his lips to the man's chest. He dragged his lips and the material lower as he inhaled Kaz's scent into his lungs. His tongue shot out, caressing Kaz's nipple as he slipped lower.

When Kaz's arms slid free of his clothing, Boston tossed it aside. Next, he went for the man's belt. Switching directions, he licked Kaz's collarbone, and he slid Kaz's zipper down. He was careful not to brush the man's erection. That was later. This was torture. Gravity took over once Kaz's pants were open, taking them to the ground. Boston pushed Kaz's underwear down the same path as his pants, dragging out the anticipation. He kept his face pressed to Kaz's chest the entire time, letting his breath fan out across the man's skin while taking in Kaz's scent. He smelled so good—so fuckable.

Kaz toed off his shoes and kicked out of the material around his ankles. Every few seconds, his palms would slide across Boston's hips, as if he forgot himself, before falling away again. Between that and Kaz's pained expression, Boston had never felt more wanted. They were in the open but out of sight. The night air caressed Boston's skin, feeding his lust. Boston pressed his body against Kaz long enough to let the man feel every hardened inch.

"Come check out the water," Boston said before stepping out of Kaz's reach and heading for the pool. Without a backward glance, he descended the steps, letting the warm water embrace him. Kaz didn't disappoint. No sooner than the water engulfed his hips, Kaz's arms encircled Boston's waist, dragging him back against in Kaz's chest. He held Boston there. His erection pressed against Boston's ass.

Kaz's lips brushed the shell of Boston's ear. "You're a tease."

Boston turned in Kaz's arms and pushed until Kaz sank down in the water. With Kaz on his knees, Boston wrapped his legs around Kaz's waist and encircled his neck, closing the final gap between them. "I'm a lot of things," Boston admitted. He sucked in a breath as their erections bumped. "But I'm not a tease," he added as he reached between them and palmed their dicks with one hand. When his eyes fell closed in pleasure, Kaz took advantage, touching his lips to Boston's. Boston opened. Their tongues brushed. The planets aligned for Boston. No one else made him feel this way. Their kiss deepened. Boston pumped faster, trying not to squirm as he jacked their cocks. They felt perfect together. The desire to let Kaz know he was important rose in Boston's chest.

He tore his mouth away, panting. "I have a confession," Boston said, sounding out of breath even to his ears.

Kaz's fingers dug into Boston's skin, as if trying to pull him closer. His lips sought Boston's neck. He didn't beg to hear Boston's big reveal. As a matter of fact, Boston wasn't sure the man was capable of hearing anything at this point. That thought didn't stop Boston from saying the words trapped in his throat.

"I've been missing you a lot between visits. A lot."

Kaz's head lifted from where he'd been nibbling at

Boston's shoulder. His eyes looked unfocused as he met Boston's gaze. His lips parted, but no sound emerged. Boston captured them before either of them said something to ruin the moment. They struggled to get closer, fighting for more. Boston blindly reached for the release Kaz's dick slipping against his promised. This time, it was Kaz who pulled away. Throwing his head back, Kaz sucked air. The cords of his neck stood out as the man's dick jumped in Boston's hand.

"Fuck. Boston."

The sound of his name on Kaz's lips as he came sent Boston flying. Even as his orgasm ripped through him, Boston didn't look away from Kaz. When Kaz's chin dropped, and he sought Boston's kiss, Boston soaked up the sweetness of his soft motions. The world might look at them and see two people who'd spent the past six months using each other for sex. Boston knew different. In moments such as this, he couldn't hide from the truth. Somewhere in the past six months, they'd transformed into something real. Maybe Boston didn't know what to do with that, but he knew he wasn't giving it up.

Chapter 4

Hot suction on his dick pulled Kaz from a dream about Boston. His lids were too heavy to lift. The corners of his mouth didn't feel the same. A smile tugged at his lips. Kaz's fingers found Boston's hair. The soft locks slipped through Kaz's fingers as he caressed the man's head. He didn't want to control Boston. The man was way too talented for Kaz's interference. Instead, Kaz focused on savoring the way Boston's palms lightly stroked his thighs. Tilting his chin up, Kaz inhaled and tried to hang on to the moment. His hips left the bed, seeking the heat of Boston's mouth. He wanted the oblivion Boston offered. Pressure built against his crown. Boston's throat tightened on his cock. Lights popped behind Kaz's closed lids. A moan vibrated from his throat. His orgasm hit. Boston didn't relent. His tongue swiped at Kaz's erection, pulling every last pop of electricity from Kaz. Boston's lips brushed Kaz's navel. Kaz held on to him, dragging him closer.

As Boston kissed a path up Kaz's body, Kaz clung to him. He tried caressing every inch of Boston's skin. The man felt so fucking delicious. Every hard line and deep valley felt like Kaz's dreams coming true. He couldn't think of a better way to start the day. In fact, Kaz didn't want to do anything else. His skin pressed against Boston's; that shit made the world go around. By the time their lips met, Kaz was ready to beg for Boston's kiss. There was something amazing about this man. Kaz didn't think the rest of the world saw it. Perhaps people liked Boston, or even wanted him for themselves, but not a single soul cared for Boston for the reasons Kaz did. Even Kaz couldn't explain the way he felt when he was with Boston—like his sins had been wiped clean. He had no past. The future didn't matter. Right now, he owned the world.

"Your breakfast is getting cold," Boston said as he attempted escape.

Kaz held tight. "You made me breakfast?"

He felt Boston shrug. "I like to cook."

"You made me breakfast, and I slept through it?"

Boston's smile turned wicked. "I enjoyed waking you up."

It had been so damn long since anyone had done so much for him. Kaz's throat tightened. He couldn't get used to this. Boston didn't do forever or even exclusivity.

"What can I do for you?" Kaz asked, needing to even the score.

Boston's smile transformed, turning sweet. "Move your ass. My pride will never recover if you hate my cooking because it's cold."

Kaz couldn't let Boston go. Not yet. "You're amazing."

"I know," Boston said with a wink and sounding as if he meant it. This time, he succeeded at pulling out of Kaz's hold.

After getting cleaned up, Kaz found Boston in the kitchen, wearing his shoes and chugging ice water.

"Going somewhere?"

Boston set his empty glass in the sink. "It's time for my morning run."

Kaz cast a glance at the table covered in enough food to feed an army. "You cooked all this and don't intend to eat?"

A wicked smile stretched Boston's lips as he closed the distance between them. "I just had my breakfast. It was delicious," Boston said before capturing Kaz's lips. It was ridiculous how easily Boston always wiped away any hint of irritation Kaz felt. "Enjoy your meal," Boston said, wiping the moisture from Kaz's bottom lip. "I'll be back before you notice I'm gone." Without another word, Boston disappeared out the door.

Kaz stared at the mountain of food. He was

ravenous. With a shrug, he tucked in. Boston had gone through the trouble. Kaz would make the best of it. He tried a little of everything. It was all amazing. By the time he was ready to burst, Kaz discovered something. Boston was wrong. Kaz noticed he was gone.

As Kaz put away the final dish, after having sealed the leftovers and washed the dishes, Boston reappeared. He was covered in sweat. Kaz's stomach growled as if he hadn't just eaten his weight in food.

Boston glanced around the kitchen. "You cleaned."

Even though Boston wasn't looking at him, and was instead filling another glass with water, Kaz still shrugged. "It was the least I could do. You cooked. I cleaned."

"I have a maid," Boston said before chugging down his water and filling his glass again. He headed for the couch with his drink. Kaz followed on his heels, unsure of what to say. It was as if Boston's mood had taken a downhill slide on his run. Kaz got it. Running would piss him off too, but he almost felt unwelcome. He chose a seat across from Boston. Boston's expression turned thunderous.

"Am I too sweaty for you?"

Kaz shook his head. "No, I—" His cellphone chirped, interrupting him. People rarely texted him.

Kaz checked the message.

Aden: *Brace yourself. The shit is about to hit the fan.*

"Liam?" Boston asked. His empty sounding voice could've meant anything.

"Aden."

Boston's scowl deepened. "How did Aden get your number?"

Kaz fought the urge to squirm. "I gave it to him when we went to lunch yesterday."

The barely suppressed rage in Boston's eyes took Kaz by surprise. "You went to lunch with Aden?"

Every thought in Kaz's head vanished. Confusion owned him. He couldn't decide why Boston pretended not to know this already. "Yes. You were sitting on my front porch with plane tickets when we got back."

He'd never seen Boston angry. Not really. He was now. Kaz didn't know how to react.

"No. I wasn't."

"Okay," Kaz said, dragging out the word and convinced Boston was fucking with him for some reason. "If you're looking to pick a fight. You could choose a different path other than pretending something didn't happen that damn well did." The more Kaz spoke, the more his anger grew. "Aden took me to lunch. When I got home, you were on my porch, demanding I spend this week with you. Tell me how you remember me getting here."

A puzzled look crossed Boston's features before his face went blank. He was doing that thing where he hid his emotions from Kaz. Kaz hated it. "I don't remember."

Boston's answer did nothing to cool Kaz's temper.

"How the fuck can you forget? It was yesterday." Boston rubbed the spot between his eyes. Kaz's gut twisted. He didn't look well. It hit Kaz—Boston wasn't fucking with him. He genuinely didn't remember. A sick feeling rose inside Kaz. "Are you okay?"

Boston rubbed his temples. "Sorry. I'm tired."

He was so pale. It seemed sudden. "It's fine. I kept you up all night."

A chuckle slipped past Boston's lips even as his eyes fell closed. For a moment, it seemed like Boston planned to set his heels on the coffee table before he slumped forward and hit the floor. Surprise kept Kaz from reacting right away. He was on his feet before he realized Boston was having a seizure. Boston also had obviously hit his head on the table on his way down because blood coated every surface surrounding him. Kaz didn't know what to do. He'd never been in this position before. Whipping his shirt over his head, he tried to stop the bleeding but couldn't do anything in the face of Boston's shaking.

Giving up, he ran for the phone and called 911.

"911. What's your emergency?"

Kaz swiped his hand over his face, trying to think, but only managing to smear Boston's blood across his forehead. "My friend is having a seizure. He hit his head on the way down and is losing a lot of blood."

"What's your address?"

For a moment, Kaz floundered. Did he know it? "I don't know," he admitted, unsure if that was true, but incapable of thinking clearly enough to pull it out of his brain.

"It's okay. We'll pull it up. Are you calling from a landline?"

"Yes."

"We'll find you."

"Thank God," Kaz breathed. "What do I need to do? I tried to stop the bleeding, but he's shaking too hard."

"If possible, turn him on his side so he doesn't choke."

It took every ounce of Kaz's strength, but he got Boston on his side. "Okay," Kaz said, letting the woman on the phone know he'd managed it. "What now?"

"Wait it out. An ambulance should be there any

minute."

"Okay."

Kaz didn't know how he managed to sound so calm. In truth, he was flipping the fuck out. Other than appearing tired and pale, Boston had seemed fine only minutes earlier. He didn't understand. Kaz didn't realize he was speaking aloud until the woman on the other line tried calming him.

"Has he had any alcohol?"

"No." Kaz was sure of it. He'd never seen the man drink. Even when Kaz did, Boston didn't. Funny, Kaz had never thought anything of it. "No. He doesn't drink."

"Any drug use?"

Kaz snorted. "Definitely not." Boston was too vain to do anything to jeopardize his looks.

"You can hang up now, sir. The ambulance is outside."

"Thank you," Kaz said, disconnecting the call as he ran to answer the door. Two paramedics stood on the other side. They were opposites in every way. A large dark-haired man and a tiny blonde woman filled the doorway. The barrel-chested of the two eyed him as if searching for injuries and reminding Kaz he'd accidentally wiped Boston's blood on his face. He tried scrubbing it off as he led them through the house. "He's in here." Nervous talking took hold of Kaz's tongue. "I've never actually seen anyone have a seizure, and he's bleeding from where he hit his head on the way down, so I didn't know what to do."

Boston wasn't shaking any longer, but he wasn't awake either, which only served to send Kaz's fear rocketing even higher.

"Why isn't he awake? Is he okay?"

"It's okay," the blonde woman said, trying to calm him. "This isn't unusual."

Kaz wasn't calmed, but she started a line of questions mirroring the ones of the 911 operator, stopping Kaz from saying anything more. It was oddly comforting. He felt like someone who knew what the fuck they were doing was there. Kaz had never felt more useless in his life. As they lifted Boston onto the gurney, Kaz grabbed a clean shirt and Boston's wallet, phone, and keys. A new set of worries set in; he didn't have any of the man's personal information—like his health insurance provider or if he even had health insurance. But Kaz was prepared to do whatever it took to help.

No one questioned him as he climbed into the back of the ambulance with Boston. The female paramedic handed him some alcohol wipes so he could scrub the blood from his hands and face as they headed for the hospital.

"Thank you," Kaz muttered. He kept his gaze locked on Boston's pale face as he tried cleaning up.

"You'll have to get his autograph for me when he wakes up," the woman joked, pulling Kaz's focus her way.

The way she was smiling went further at reassuring Kaz than anything had. Surely she wouldn't seem this unconcerned if Boston was in danger of dying. Kaz returned her smile. "He's a showboat, so I'm sure he won't mind."

"I can hear you," Boston said, making Kaz's head snap around.

Kaz almost crowed in relief at the sight of Boston's gorgeous eyes. Before he could say a word, the paramedic blocked Kaz's sight of him by shining a penlight in Boston's eyes.

"Do you remember what happened, Mr. Tyler?"

"No."

Hearing Boston's answer broke Kaz's heart.

"You had a seizure and hit your head on the coffee table," the paramedic explained. "You've lost quite a bit of blood. They'll have to run a few tests and x-rays, I imagine, but I've seen you fight. You've got a hard head."

Boston chuckled but didn't say anything else. It took every ounce of Kaz's restraint not to push the woman out of his way. He wanted to check on Boston for himself. The man had scared Kaz shitless.

Obviously either assessing Boston or trying to get gossip, Kaz wasn't sure which, she continued asking questions. "Can you tell me your full name?"

"Boston Wayne Tyler."

"Good. How old are you, Boston?"

"Thirty-three."

While nodding and making notes, the paramedic didn't let up. "Can you tell me your friend's name?"

"Kaz Sobong."

Other than sounding weak, Boston appeared okay. Seemingly satisfied, the woman finally moved aside, allowing Kaz to get closer. The instant he could, Kaz took Boston's hand. He had no fucks to give about anyone's opinion. Kaz hated this.

"You scared the hell out of me. How are you feeling?"

Boston's eyes fell closed, but he smiled. "Not quite the thrill you were looking for this week, huh?"

Kaz brushed off his question. "Seriously, how do

you feel?"

A dimple appeared at the corner of Boston's mouth. "Like a million bucks."

"Liar," Kaz growled.

One blue eye popped open. "Do you know how a million bucks feels?"

In spite of himself, Kaz fought back a smile. "No."

"Fucking heavy," Boston said, making Kaz's shoulders shake with laughter. Damn, this man. The pressure of Boston's fingers through his increased as Boston squeezed his hand. Kaz wasn't sure if he wanted to laugh or cry. For real, it had been one hell of a day.

*

Liam: *Tell me it's not true. Tell me you're not dating Boston.*

Kaz: *I don't have time for this right now. Please enjoy your honeymoon.*

Liam: *People have been blowing Gunnar's phone up all day. Are you with him right now?*

Kaz: *I love you. Enjoy your time with your husband.*

In the past, telling Liam he loved him was the fastest way to get Liam to stop talking to him. Unfortunately, it didn't work today.

Liam: *Tell me the rumors aren't true, and I'll get*

back to enjoying my husband. I don't want you to get hurt.

Kaz: *Seriously, I don't have time for this. You have a new life now. Let me have mine.*

For good measure, Kaz turned off his phone. He couldn't deal with anything else right now with Boston in the hospital.

Boston had a hard time staying awake. Kaz stayed as quiet as possible, letting him rest. He knew from experience nothing was worse than feeling bad while having to entertain people. The shaking in his stomach that began when Boston collapsed hadn't subsided. To counter it, Kaz kept his hands balled into fists as he watched Boston sleep. Boston looked peaceful. He didn't stir or snore. The man's chest rose and fell, like a child tucked into bed for the night. Kaz wanted to lower the railing and climb in beside him. He wanted to press his ear to Boston's chest, reassuring himself that Boston's heart beat steady. Mostly, Kaz wanted to hold Boston and squelch the fear inside him. He didn't know what was wrong with Boston or if Boston knew. All Kaz knew was he hadn't been through anything this horrific before and he was scared. All the way to his bones. The idea of Boston dying, leaving Kaz to face an empty life, was chilling.

A light knock landing on the door was all the warning Kaz got before the ER's attending physician strolled in. The short, brown-haired man wore a white lab coat with the hospital's name and logo stitched above the pocket at his chest. He shook Kaz's hand before reaching to shake Boston's, making Kaz realize Boston was awake.

"I hear you've had an exciting day, Mr. Tyler. I'm Dr. Tate. Do you have any history of seizures?"

Boston nodded. "I suffered a brain injury a few years back, and it caused me to develop epilepsy."

"Are you taking medication to control the seizures?"

"Yes."

The questions kept coming. "Did you skip a dose or have any alcohol?"

Boston shook his head. "I overdid it. Sometimes, I go so long between episodes, I forget I'm not who I used to be."

Dr. Tate nodded. "It happens. I looked over all your tests, and you lost a bit of blood but not so much I think you need an infusion. Just rest. I'm going to send you home, but you need to set up an appointment with your physician for next week. In the meantime, drink lots of fluids and get plenty of sleep. Those things are important to your health. No driving for at least two days." The doctor switched his attention Kaz's way. "He'll need someone to sign, saying they'll be responsible for his care for the next twenty-four hours. Are you okay to do that?"

Kaz nodded. "It's no problem."

"I'll get the paperwork together. Things move slow around here sometimes. It may take a while. Just sit back and relax."

The second they were alone, Kaz focused on Boston. He had so many questions he didn't know where to start. Boston wouldn't meet his gaze. Kaz didn't let that deter him.

"You suffered a brain injury? When? How?"

At his questions, Boston finally looked Kaz's way. The dark circles under his eyes made Kaz feel like shit for pushing. Sometimes, he forgot he was nothing more than a booty call to Boston. He had no right. "Sorry," Kaz muttered. "It's none of my business."

Boston's features softened. "Why would you say that? You're here. Of course it's your business. I took too many shots to the head during my boxing career. That's why I'm retiring."

In spite of Boston's nonchalant tone, his eyes said something different. He'd lost an intricate part of himself. "That journalist last night was digging to know if you were retiring, but you didn't confirm it. Wait. You told the doctor the brain injury occurred a few years back, and you've still been boxing. Is that even legal?"

Boston shook his head. "If they'd known, they wouldn't have let me compete. Looking back on things, I realize I was in denial. Part of me honestly thought I could keep fighting as long as no one found out."

"But you were dating Gunnar a few years ago. Surely he would've said something. He doesn't seem the type to let anyone get hurt."

A bitter smile touched Boston's lips. "Exactly. So, he had to go. I chose fame over everything, babe," Boston said, sounding tired. "That title was my dream. After it was mine, I spent my time boasting about there being no one worthy of a challenge, putting off the inevitable. I knew I was on borrowed time. It should've been Gunnar's all along. I should've stopped fighting long before I did." Boston's slur worsened the longer he spoke. His eyes slipped closed. "All's right now. I can fade away. No one needs to know how long this has been happening. Don't tell, 'kay?"

"I won't tell," Kaz promised, even though he was certain Boston was already asleep.

Chapter 5

No matter how much Kaz argued and begged, he couldn't get Boston to relax. Not really. The best he'd managed was to get Boston to stay in bed until lunchtime. Boston argued his hospital visit the day before had already stolen too much quality time from them. That was why Kaz was sitting across the kitchen island from Boston, watching him chop vegetables for a salad he swore would ruin Kaz for all other salads. In Kaz's opinion, that wasn't too tall of a feat. A salad was a salad as far as he was concerned. Food preparation seemed to make Boston happy, so he let the man fix their lunch without argument.

As he stared at the stitches at Boston's temple, worry ate at Kaz's gut. What if he hadn't been here? Why did Boston keep acting as if nothing happened? "I have to get back to work this weekend. Two weekends off in a row is too many where I work. I can't make it three."

Boston glanced up from chopping. His smile tightened Kaz's throat. He wasn't bothered by the announcement. "Okay."

"That's it? Just okay?"

A line appeared between Boston's eyes before clearing away. "I bought your tickets. It's not like I didn't know when you were headed home."

A growl crawled up Kaz's throat. He knew he wasn't being clear, but he couldn't understand Boston's nonchalance. "Is there someone who can stay with you after I'm gone?"

Boston's expression couldn't have screamed confusion any more than it did. "What? If this is your way of asking if I'm seeing other people, you could just ask that, you know?"

Aggravation ruled Kaz. It was as if Boston purposely misunderstood or was dodging. "That's not what I'm asking." Because Hell would freeze before Kaz asked that. "What happens if you have another episode and you're alone?"

The confusion cleared from Boston's face. His expression went blank. "I'll do what I always do—stay where I land until my head clears and then go to bed until I'm feeling better."

"Do what you always..." Kaz's temper snapped. "Are you fucking kidding me? You could die. What if you hit your head again? You need someone staying with you full-time. A family member." Kaz swallowed before adding, "Another friend."

"Is that what we are?" Boston asked, using his most mocking tone. It did nothing for Kaz's temper.

"Goddamn it, why are you making light of this? Next time, you might bleed out. You could hit your head and die." Every time he said the words, it tasted like ash in his mouth, but Kaz couldn't drive home his point without them.

In an unexpected burst of anger, Boston slammed the knife down on the counter with enough force to snap the handle. The loud bang rang from the kitchen walls. "There is no one," Boston yelled, taking Kaz by surprise with his show of emotion. "Take a look around, Kaz. There is no one."

"Not even a single family member?" Kaz asked, but the fire had bled from his argument in the face of Boston's conviction.

A derisive smile touched Boston's lips. "You can't have both, babe. It's either fame or love. I chose fame, and it was a full-on soul trade. With every fight I won and autograph I signed, another person slipped away. Sometimes it was because I wasn't around. Other times, I pushed them out of my way. But the game is always the same—no one wants me for me, only for what I can do for them. So, yeah, I suppose I'll die alone one day. That's the choice I made." Boston's smile

73

turned brittle. Kaz hated it. "It was worth it," Boston added. "After all, it got me you."

For a full thirty seconds, Kaz considered punching Boston in his perfect face. The rage passed as quickly as it came. He got Boston. This was how he protected his heart. They were so alike. Someone had to be the one to drop kick their pride. "I'd never seen a boxing match in my life until you fought Gunnar. Before you hit me in front of Gunnar's apartment, I'd never heard your name. The first time I kissed you, I didn't care at all about the fame," Kaz said, laying it all on the line. "I want you for you."

Boston snorted. "You want me because I'm convenient."

"No," Kaz said, admitting it all. "Everyone is convenient where I work. I'm propositioned every night at least five times. It's you I want. You're the only person who makes me feel alive. Come home with me." The offer slipped from Kaz before he'd known he'd make it. He didn't take it back.

Instead of answering, Boston attacked his claims. "That's not the kind of convenient I meant. It's Liam you want. There will never be anyone else for you, especially me—the man who hurt the only person you'll ever love. But you keep letting me in because I don't threaten that. You can hang on to him for the rest of your life without being alone, because you have me, and I matter not at all to anyone."

Kaz couldn't make his throat work in the face of Boston showing his heart. There was so much bitterness in Boston's expression, Kaz didn't know how he'd missed it before now. Once the floodgates opened, Boston didn't stop.

"Did you know, the only time you smile is when you talk about him? I can make you moan and beg. Maybe I can pull a few minutes of ecstasy from you, but I don't make you happy. You don't love me. It'll always only be Liam. I'm not your other half. That's not what this is. It's pity and I don't want it."

Boston turned away and leaned against the counter. Kaz watched his shoulders heave as he switched positions, crossing his arms over his chest before uncrossing them and bracing his palms on the counter on either side of him. Boston stared down at his feet, obviously attempting to call his temper under control. Kaz didn't know if he could deny every word Boston spoke, but he knew Boston was wrong about a few things. Closing the distance between them, Kaz didn't wait for permission. He wrapped his arms around Boston and held on. Kaz's body reacted exactly as he knew it would; it burned. His dick stirred along with the butterflies in his stomach because it was Boston. He couldn't explain it. In fact, he'd never wanted it, but Boston did something for him no one else did. Kaz forced Boston's chin up, making the man hold his gaze.

"Tell me all about how I don't want you," Kaz taunted, guiding Boston's hand to his erection. His eyes fell closed for a second as Boston kneaded his cock through his jeans. His lust gave him courage. When Kaz's eyes reopened and his gaze met Boston's gorgeous blue stare, the words poured from Kaz as if his heart couldn't be broken. "You're so fucking wrong, Boston. I catch myself smiling like an idiot all the time, every time I think of you. I try smothering it because I know you'll never care about me. It's not that I don't love you, it's that you'll never love me." Boston blinked as if trying to process the words, but Kaz wasn't ready to hear anything Boston had to say, especially since Kaz didn't doubt Boston wouldn't speak to him again after today. "For over six months, you've been coming around, stealing pieces of me. Fuck you for trying to tell me how I feel. You don't get to choose for me. If I'm not smiling, it's your goddamn fault because I know you'll be gone in a few days again, and I never know if it's for good this time. I'm the unwanted one in this equation. I'm the one who knows for certain you'll never think of me as your other half. You'll never think of anyone that way. We're all just playthings to you. Do you have any idea how much—" Boston's mouth slammed down on Kaz's with enough force Kaz tasted blood, cutting off Kaz's words. His tongue stroked Kaz's, stealing away Kaz's rage. He did it again, wiping the thoughts from Kaz's mind. Boston's fingers dug into Kaz's back as he pulled Kaz closer, leaving no room between them.

"They'll hate you," Boston said as he changed direction, coming at Kaz from a different angle.

Kaz accepted it because he couldn't resist until he couldn't stand the curiosity any longer. "Who'll hate me?" he asked against Boston's lips.

Boston snagged Kaz's hair and pulled, exposing Kaz's throat. His teeth nipped at Kaz's skin as he answered. "Everyone. They'll all hate you loving me."

Finding the drawstring of Boston's shorts, Kaz tugged, loosening them before delving his hand inside. He palmed Boston's dick, letting his arousal win. "I don't care. Let them hate."

Kaz's jeans loosened beneath Boston's touch. He dragged the material down Kaz's hips. Cool air brushed his erection. "You will. Eventually, it'll matter to you. But I'm selfish," Boston said as he kicked out his shorts and underwear. "I'll let them drag your name through the gutter just to be with you. That's not love, Kaz. Love would be me letting you go." Bracing himself against the counter, Boston let Kaz lift his feet from the floor. With Boston's legs wrapped around his waist, Kaz licked his fingers before stretching Boston's hole. He watched the man's every reaction. Boston was the most responsive person he'd ever touched. He was a sexual being. With his lips parted and his head thrown back, Boston rode Kaz's fingers.

"Jesus, Kaz." He bit his bottom lip as if holding back the words racing through his head. Kaz didn't want that. He needed to hear every thought.

He shoved three fingers inside, ruthlessly plugging Boston's ass. A cry fell from Boston's gorgeous lips. "Hang on."

That was all the warning Kaz gave before shifting his hold and falling to his knees. With Boston's thighs on his shoulders, Kaz grabbed Boston's ass cheeks, spreading them wide as he dove in. He tongued Boston's gorgeous hole before dragging his tongue upward and taking the man's balls between his lips. He sucked lightly before licking a path up Boston's erection. Opening his jaw wide, he did his best to keep Boston from spilling into the floor as he let the man openly fuck his willing mouth. Boston was strong with lots of stamina. He barely broke a sweat as he used the edge of the counter to balance himself as he pumped inside Kaz's throat. Kaz loved the taste of Boston's dick. He sucked and licked, trying to savor every inch. The sound of Boston's moans was music to his ears. His spit ran down his chin, coating everything and easing Boston's ride. It was messy and raw just the way Kaz loved it. His eyes watered and his throat burned. It was heaven. Boston's muscles jerked as semen filled Kaz's mouth. The thick, salty fluid coated his tongue, ran down his chin, and dripped onto Boston's stomach. Kaz was blind, deaf, and mute to everything as he swiped his hand through the mess. He used it to finger Boston's ass, tearing more cries from the man in his arms. Boston's greedy asshole tugged at Kaz's fingers, making his dick jealous.

Incapable of standing another second of the torment of his dick screaming, Kaz shifted back to his feet. Without waiting for permission, he fisted his cock and shoved his way inside Boston's ass. Boston cried out. His dick twitched on his stomach as if seeking even more pleasure. Kaz stared down at Boston's cock,

79

still glistening with his saliva, as he fucked Boston's ass—hard. This man was so goddamn perfect for him. They were each other's second chance. Kaz's eyes burned. He couldn't lift his gaze to meet Boston's. His heart was too raw and exposed. The heat pulling on his cock, sending sparks of pleasure through him, and trying to relieve the pressure beating at his crown; it had nothing on the way Boston affected the rest of Kaz's body. He stole his breath. Made his heart race. His beauty hurt Kaz's eyes, and his laugh seduced Kaz's ears. When they kissed, Kaz tasted salvation. This man could not die and leave him. It didn't matter if Boston didn't love him.

He lifted his gaze, showing Boston his heart. "I love you."

Boston's lips parted. His shock was the most beautiful thing Kaz had ever seen because he knew then—Boston believed.

"Come back to Key Largo with me." Kaz heard the offer leave his lips as if someone else had spoken. The moment the words hung between them, they felt right. Kaz wanted this. "Come home with me. Let me take care of you."

Boston pushed at Kaz's chest until he took a step back, giving Boston his space and allowing his feet to slip to the floor. As soon as he was free, Boston snatched his clothes from the floor and swiped at his skin, wiping away their mess. He didn't look at Kaz as he responded.

"You want me to walk away from all this— everything I've worked for, to come stay with you in your tiny two-bedroom house, and let you take care of me as if I'm a child?"

For a full minute, Kaz didn't know what to say. His mind was still fogged with lust and Boston's rage didn't fit the moment. Kaz glanced around at everything Boston had built for himself. The blank walls and empty shelves held no appeal. It didn't bother him that Boston was putting money between them for the first time. He'd known that shit would eventually happen. Boston had always been too far out of his league. But it fucking killed him that Boston would choose this cold house over him.

He met Boston's gaze. "I'm asking you to let me take care of you as if you're the man I love." Because it was all Kaz had to offer, Kaz didn't hold back. He couldn't argue he could give Boston any sort of life or that he was worth more than what Boston had built, but he could love him.

Boston smirked. Kaz's gut twisted. "We've got a

good thing, Kaz. Don't ruin it by trying to make it more than it is."

He couldn't let this go. Kaz had already put his heart on the line. If he meant nothing to Boston, Kaz needed the man to demolish him now, before Kaz lost more of himself to someone who would never care about him. "So what is this between us, then?"

Boston snorted, twisting the knife in Kaz's chest. "We're two friends who occasionally fuck. Nothing more. See? No reason for you to worry over me." Boston turned away, heading for the bedroom and taking Kaz's heart with him. The desire to chase Boston down the hall passed as quickly as it came. He'd asked for it, and Boston had delivered. Instead of begging, as his heart screamed for Kaz to do, he straightened his clothes, washed his hands, and picked up chopping where Boston left off. Kaz's flight didn't leave for a few more days. This was the last of his time in New Orleans with Boston. No doubt, the man wouldn't bother with him again after this trip. That didn't mean Kaz had to spend the remainder of his stay angry and hurting. There'd be plenty of time for that when he got home—when he was alone. The way he always was.

Boston's arms encircled Kaz's waist and his lips settled on Kaz's nape. Kaz kept his gaze locked on his duty. The backs of his eyes burned and his nose stung. But Kaz was finished being weak. He'd taken a chance and lost. No going back.

"I didn't mean any of that." Kaz stopped breathing at Boston's whispered confession. "I don't know why I do the things I do or say the things I say." Kaz knew. Boston was protecting himself. Like him, Boston had been the bad guy for so long, he didn't know how to be anything else. "You know I love your tiny house in Key Largo. It's perfect because there's no place for you to hide from me." His arms tightened around Kaz. "We're not just friends and this isn't just sex. If you go out with Aden again, I'll kill you both." Kaz's heart beat so fast there was no way Boston couldn't feel it racing. "I'm a grown man who doesn't need a nursemaid. If you want to have a conversation about moving in together, I'm willing, but not because of this."

Kaz kept chopping vegetables, incapable of thinking of a single response. Boston set his hand on top of Kaz's, stopping him. "Please stop. You know cooking is my job, and—quite frankly—you're fucking it up."

A snort escaped Kaz. "I'm chopping. That's it. How could I have possibly fucked that up?"

"You just are," Boston said on a chuckle. He pried

the knife from Kaz's hand and turned Kaz in his arms. "Walk away before you do any more damage." Now that Kaz couldn't avoid Boston's gaze, he couldn't look away. Boston wasn't talking about the vegetables.

"No."

Boston eyed him as if assessing his seriousness before responding. "Then tell me what you want."

Kaz refused to back down. "You. Every night from now on."

"I like my couch better than yours."

Biting back a smile, Kaz nodded. "We can use yours instead."

"My bed too."

It was hard, but Kaz kept his expression blank. "Okay."

"And my TV is bigger than yours."

Kaz chewed on his bottom lip. He could feel his smile winning. "We'll move mine to the bedroom."

"Deal." Boston moved in closer until they were chest to chest. "I left you hanging and you're not even the tiniest bit mad."

Kaz shook his head. It didn't matter.

"Any other man would be furious."

In his confusion, Kaz's eyebrows drew together. "What kind of men do you hang out with? Being with you isn't about the sex, Boston."

Boston's gaze dropped to Kaz's mouth before returning to hold Kaz's stare. It was the smallest gesture, but it had Kaz's body on fire. "The erection between us says something different."

A low chuckle rumbled from Kaz's chest. Boston felt so damn good in his arms. He was like holding on to a warm breeze. Kaz spent every second amazed he'd pulled off snagging Boston while basking in the man's caress. Still, Kaz expected Boston would slip away any second, leaving him to wonder if any of this had been real. "The erection between us knows what you can do for it, but my dick doesn't control me."

Boston's expression turned serious. "I want to control you."

Kaz wasn't surprised by Boston's confession. Boston was a force of nature. Bending people to his will was in his blood. What shocked Kaz was his body's reaction. His breath left his lungs on a whoosh and butterflies stirred in his stomach.

Boston's fingertips skimmed down Kaz's spine. The breathing situation worsened. "You're not running away."

Kaz shook his head.

"You should. I'm being one hundred percent honest

with you. I'll take over your life."

A pant escaped Kaz. His gaze zeroed in on Boston's mouth. He needed to watch every sexy word leaving Boston's lips.

"Pretty soon, you won't recognize yourself. You'll wonder when you changed or if you care. I can make you not care."

He already didn't care.

"Do you really want me in your bed every night?"

Kaz licked his lips. He was more turned on than he'd ever been in his life. "Yes."

"Do you want me bad enough to quit your job?"

Kaz's gaze snapped from Boston's mouth to his eyes. He held the man's gaze. Boston was serious. "What?"

Boston's face hardened. "You heard me. I see your face when people ask where you work. You hate it. Not to mention, you made a huge mistake by telling me you're propositioned five times a night. Should I sit home every weekend and wonder?" A smirk touched Boston's lips. "That's not in me. I'm jealous and possessive. I'll make you sorry."

"A few minutes ago, we struck a deal. Now, you're changing the rules."

Boston shrugged. "I do that."

"What am I supposed to do for money?"

Laughter flashed in Boston's eyes. "You're supposed to trust me. Blindly. Without question."

Maybe Kaz had completely lost his mind, but he did. "Can I give my two weeks' notice? Jeff is a nice guy. I don't want to leave him hanging."

Boston dipped his chin. "I can live with that. How hungry are you?"

Against his will, Kaz's gaze dropped to Boston's mouth again. "For food? Not at all."

"I love the way you look at me," Boston said as if confessing a dirty secret. He immediately changed tack again. "What about attention? Are you hungry for that?"

"I'm always starved for attention."

Boston's arms tightened around him.

The backs of Kaz's eyes burned. His throat swelled. Why did he bare his soul every time Boston asked him to?

"I have what you need," Boston said so low Kaz had to strain to hear. It was true. Boston had everything Kaz required—like oxygen.

"I know you do," Kaz said, his voice coming out thick. "That wasn't supposed to happen."

A smile lit Boston's face. "But it did, and now what

can you do? Nothing," Boston said without giving Kaz time to answer. "And now you'll tell me your deepest desires," Boston said, pulling away and heading for the kitchen table. After snagging a chair and bringing it closer, Boston climbed on top of it, standing tall.

Kaz rushed to his side and grabbed hold of Boston's hips. "Don't do that. You just got out of the hospital. You shouldn't be climbing on things."

Boston smirked. "Funny how you weren't worried about my hospital stay when you were fucking me on the counter. Nope," Boston said in a booming voice. "I'm here to give you all the over-the-top attention you need. Your wish is my command. Tell me your deepest desires," Boston said, keeping up his announcer's voice. "What's your first wish?"

It was impossible not to get sucked into Boston's game. Kaz's cheeks ached from smiling. Boston was serious. He'd do whatever Kaz wanted. The knowledge was empowering. Delicious possibilities raced through Kaz's head.

"How many wishes do I get?"

"As many as you'd like," Boston swore, still using his obnoxious announcer's voice.

"Hmmm," Kaz said, playing along. "How about a kiss?"

"That's too easy." Boston leaned down and pressed a quick kiss to Kaz's lips before going back to his Superman pose. "What else?"

"When you're done here, I want to stay in bed with you the rest of the day."

"Done. Next."

Kaz was getting into the spirit of things. "Let's cancel my flight and drive back together."

Boston nodded. "I need to do that anyhow, so I can move my stuff. Come on. Take this seriously. Ask me for something big."

"Tell me three things about you nobody else knows," Kaz demanded without having to think about it. That was what he wanted more than anything—to know Boston better than anyone on the planet. To be special.

"You're still too easy, and to be fair—thanks to my unexpected trip to the hospital—you already know something about me no one else does. However, I did say you could have anything, so I'll still give you three."

Kaz knew he would. Boston was always straight with him.

"One," Boston said, holding up one finger. "I'm terrified of spiders. Seriously, you'd better get that shit if one gets in our house or I'll never sleep there again.

We'll have to burn that shit down."

He'd called it their house. Kaz couldn't stop smiling. "Just call me the bug man."

"Good," Boston said, sounding relieved. "Two, when I was twelve, I stole a lighter and a pack of cigarettes from this old man at the flea market. Don't ask; my grandparents loved the flea market. We went every weekend. Anyhow, I had it in my head that'd I'd be cool and take up smoking. Instead, between the horrible guilt over my thievery and the nasty smoke, I was so sick I ended up puking all day. When I turned eighteen, I went back to that market and the old man was still setting up there. When he wasn't looking, I left fifty bucks by his register."

Kaz stared up at Boston, still clinging to the man's hips and hanging on every word. He loved this man. It sat on his chest, making Kaz wonder how he'd ever denied the sensation for what it was.

"I've never told anyone that story. Actually, I have hundreds of stories I've never told anyone, if you want more than three?"

Kaz had to clear his throat to speak. "I want every single one. Today, I'll settle for one more."

Boston's hands covered Kaz's. His expression turned serious. "There's one that stands out above the rest."

"Okay," Kaz said, pushing the word past his rapidly drying throat.

"The day I propositioned you, I was holding that ice to your face and watching you while you kept your eyes closed. There was this rock sitting in my stomach. I was the reason for the bruises on your face. It was my fault Liam and Gunnar were on the other side of the door, fighting for their relationship. Sometimes, it's like I'm a disease. I hated myself more that day than I had in a long time and that's saying a lot. Yet, you were still trusting me to take care of you—like I wasn't a complete loss." Boston licked his lips but still held Kaz's gaze. The nervous gesture had Kaz's heart turning over in his chest. This was what he wanted. The real Boston. "I have a feeling I've been in love with you way longer than you've loved me. You saved me. Can we go to bed now?"

The vulnerable note to Boston's voice had Kaz pulling the man down from the chair and into his arms.

"I thought you'd never ask."

Chapter 6

Settling into Kaz's had been no hardship. He still hadn't moved more than half his things. Boston didn't miss any of it. Each night, he drifted off to sleep with Kaz's head resting on his chest. Every morning, he awoke with Kaz's ass pressed against his crotch. He hadn't thought himself capable of settling down with anyone. With Kaz, everything was so fucking simple. They didn't fight. The place never seemed too small for the two of them. Boston had gone from always being alone to never being out of Kaz's sight, and it was intoxicating. The more he got of Kaz, the more Boston wanted. He'd never felt greedier in his life and that was saying something.

"Funny story," Kaz said as he stepped out of the bedroom and filled Boston with anticipation. "I tried to pay our mortgage today, and there wasn't one."

Boston swiped his tongue over his teeth, trying not to smile. "That's odd."

"Very," Kaz agreed. "You wouldn't know anything about that, would you?"

"Happy mistake?" Boston suggested.

Kaz moved closer. A dimple appeared in his cheek

before disappearing again. It was obvious he was trying to hide his happiness. Yeah, so Boston had paid off the man's mortgage. It hadn't been huge and barely made a blip in Boston's bank account. Kaz's happiness, though, that shit was priceless.

"So it's your opinion I should chalk this up to an odd blessing?"

"Absolutely," Boston said. He sat forward on the couch and set his elbows on his knees, needing to get a hair closer to Kaz. "I need to talk to you," Boston said, snagging Kaz's waist the second Kaz was close enough and pulling the man down into his lap.

Kaz switched positions and straddled Boston's hips, moving in close. "All right."

Without thought, Boston's hands moved to Kaz's back. He massaged, loving the way his man felt beneath his palms. "My house sold."

"Damn. That was fast."

"Yeah."

Kaz chewed on his bottom lip for a second. "Does that mean you're ready to move out of my tiny two-bedroom house? Is that why you paid off the mortgage?"

Boston hated when Kaz talked down about his shit. Yeah, he'd called Kaz's home tiny at one point, but it had nothing to do with Kaz's house and everything to do with Boston's insecurities. "No. I told you I love it here. You can't hide from me in this place. Although I will have to find someplace for all my shit. We need to go through my things and figure out what we want to keep, if there's a place for it, and what we'll do with whatever is left over." He swiped his hand through the air. "But I digress. I wanted to talk to you about my plans for the money I'm making off the sale."

Kaz looked worried. Boston couldn't decide why. "Okay."

He massaged Kaz's hips between his hands, hoping to ease the man's worry. "Before I started winning every match, I used to prepare these awesome healthy meals while trying to stay in shape. You know how it is when you're working out all the time. There's nothing you'd like better than to eat all the food. Anyhow, I got really good at it."

"I know. You've cooked for me several times."

"That's my second career choice," Boston admitted like ripping off a bandage. He wasn't used to baring his soul to anyone, but Kaz was different. "I want to open a restaurant, serving healthy but delicious food."

Kaz nodded. His expression gave nothing away. "Kay Largo could use some new restaurants. You have to go all the way to Miami for most things."

"So, what do you think?"

A smile exploded across Kaz's face. "I think you're amazing at everything you do and owning a restaurant wouldn't be any different."

Butterflies stirred in Boston's stomach. Since meeting Kaz, he'd found new excitement in life. Kaz always sent flutters through Boston, but in this case, it was nerves. "Here's the thing, I don't want it to be mine alone. I want you to be a part of it."

Kaz nodded, looking thoughtful. "How so? I quit my job. My savings is almost empty. It's not as if I can buy in. I have nothing to offer."

A hint of irritation ran through Boston. "First off, there's no reason for your savings to be almost empty. You have me for that. Don't make me get your bank info from your mom so I can deposit money directly into your account. Secondly, I'm not talking about buying in. I need your time, help, and support. Basically, I'm asking you to be my partner in this."

"I'm your partner in all things."

"Awesome," Boston said, never meaning anything more. He loved that Kaz thought of himself as Boston's partner in life. I have an appointment to see the building I want to buy in thirty minutes."

Kaz's lips parted. Boston wanted to laugh at Kaz's surprise. "Whoa. You don't let any grass grow under your feet. Do you?"

"I'm a man who knows what he wants," Boston said, tugging Kaz down for a kiss. The moment their lips met, Boston forgot what they were talking about. He forgot everything. The pressure of Kaz's mouth against his, sharing air; it was the reason Boston got up every morning. "Kaz," Boston whispered against his lips. Kaz's muscles tensed as if he meant to move away. Without thought, Boston tightened his hold. "Don't stop."

Kaz groaned. "I have to. You have an appointment."

Boston's shoulders fell at the reminder. "Fuck." After letting his head fall back against the couch, Boston stared at Kaz and tried to get his body back under control. There wasn't enough time to play. With his arms braced against the couch on either side of Boston, Kaz stared back. Emotion clogged Boston's throat. He didn't want to move. If he could, he'd stay as they were all day. A million times he'd gone over every second he'd spent with Kaz, and he couldn't find the one that had changed him. Somewhere along the line, Boston had lost all desire to do anything other than what he did right now. Being with Kaz, it was enough. For the first time in his life, he felt full. There was no hunger for more. "I love you."

Kaz's sexy lips shaped into a smile. "I love you too."

The roaring need was back—that hunger to give Kaz the world, making them even. He had to cement his place in Kaz's life. The mortgage was only the first in a long line of things Boston had planned. One day soon, Kaz would wake up and wonder when Boston became such a fundamental piece of his life and why he couldn't get away. It had to be done. He was living on borrowed time in this relationship. Soon the novelty would wear off for Kaz, and he'd see Boston for the terrible person he was.

"Damn. You spoil me."

The way Kaz's face screwed up in confusion made Boston want to laugh.

"Okay," Kaz said, dragging out the word. "You paid off the house, cook every meal, and every time we leave, cleaning fairies show up. I haven't figured out how you're pulling that one off yet. How am I doing the spoiling here?"

Kaz made him feel like he could be perfect. Boston had never been flawless in anyone's eyes before. A smile pulled at the corners of Boston's mouth as he answered Kaz's question. "You woke up today."

*

You woke up today. Those words ran through Kaz's head like a mantra all the way to the restaurant. Who said shit like that? For sure, he'd never had anyone make him feel so necessary. Kaz could barely breathe from the weight of his astonishment. Kaz had been staring into Boston's eyes when Boston made the claim. He'd meant those words. Kaz didn't deserve them, but he wanted to. Boston did so much for him. Kaz was just there. He didn't have money or any smooth lines. All Kaz had was love.

It seemed no sooner than they got on the road, Boston turned into the parking lot of an old restaurant Kaz knew well. He couldn't hide his surprise.

"Damn. You want to buy Momma Dee's?"

Boston's expression was priceless. Kaz had zero control over the excitement racing through him. As soon as Boston had mentioned opening a restaurant, the old Momma Dee's had popped into Kaz's head. He'd never dreamed Boston had actually chosen that spot. Kaz felt the need to explain his over-the-top reaction.

"There used to be a restaurant here called Momma Dee's. Even before I moved here, back when I was a teenager, my parents used to bring me here all the time. It was my favorite place to eat."

Boston winked. "I know. I went by your parents' shop the other night while you were working your final shift. When I told your mom about my plan, she told me about this place."

"You've been visiting my parents again," Kaz said, hearing the amazement in his own voice and incapable of stopping it.

Boston kept talking as if Kaz hadn't said a word. "Plus, this place is only five minutes from the house. Convenience matters to me since I don't ever want to be far away from you again."

A woman wearing a flowered dress who looked exactly like Kaz would've pictured a realtor looking waved at them from the door. Boston opened his door and set one foot on the ground. Kaz followed suit. Before he could push from the car, Boston snagged his arm, stopping him. When Kaz looked over, he swore Boston's heart was in his eyes.

"By the way, I like visiting with your parents. Mine no longer care to see me. You have no idea what it's like to have people happy to see you, when no one has cared if you lived or died in years. Be honest about this place," Boston said, rapidly jumping topics as if Kaz's heart wasn't breaking on his behalf. "Don't tell me you love it for nostalgic reasons. If you hate it because it's sat empty too long, we can find a different spot or build from scratch." Without waiting for his agreement, Boston pressed a quick kiss to Kaz's lips and jumped from the car. It took Kaz a little longer to get his legs working. Boston never sat down and simply bared his soul. He said things in bursts, giving Kaz insights he hadn't known he wanted. If Boston needed someone to be excited to see him, Kaz wouldn't let him down.

Boston stood in the doorway, waiting, as if he had no intention of stepping inside until Kaz was at his side. It was a small gesture. Kaz picked up the pace, savoring the knowledge he was important to Boston. The instant he was at Boston's side, Boston linked fingers with him and stepped through the door. The place was everything Kaz remembered—if not a little dirty. Actually, it was a lot dirty and falling apart, but it was bigger than Kaz remembered. They wouldn't have an issue of customers having to wait a long time to be seated if they were busy.

Kaz listened with half an ear as Boston explained his plan to open a restaurant centered around a healthy diet. Of course, he didn't intend to market it that way. Boston said something about food for champions and Kaz wandered off. First, he stooped down and inspected the floor before moving on to the walls. For the most part, the structure looked sound, but the floors needed replacing.

"So, what do you think?" Boston asked, startling Kaz. He'd thought the man was still chit-chatting with the realtor. Boston was light on his feet and sneaky as fuck when he put his mind to it.

"It's sound," Kaz said, trying to hide the way his heart raced. He hated when anyone sneaked up on him. "Of course, it needs a proper inspection, but from what I can tell, it's still in great shape. What do you think?"

"It has a bar."

The excitement in Boston's tone had a smile stretching Kaz's lips. "Baby, you don't even drink."

"I want to turn it into a milkshake bar. You know, like the old timey ice cream counters."

Kaz was ready to say yes to buying the place based on Boston's enthusiasm alone, but Boston had asked him to be honest. To be fair, he cast a real look around the building, attempting to picture the place as Boston wanted it to be. He could see it.

"I could see us here. Barring a proper inspection, of course."

Kaz had to bite his lip to hold in his laughter at Boston's childlike grin. He was happy. Kaz was complete. "I'll go talk money."

With Boston back to chatting business, Kaz made his way outside. He walked the perimeter, trying to think of a way to personalize the place. A third car pulled into the parking lot, snagging Kaz's attention. The man who stepped from the car looked familiar. Kaz couldn't place where they'd met before.

"Mr. Sobong, it's nice to see you again."

Kaz had nothing. Zero things about the man fit any memory Kaz could dredge up. There was only a vague sense of dislike. Luckily, Boston stepped out, saving Kaz from admitting his loss.

"Daniel, I'm glad you could make it."

When Boston and Daniel shook hands, everything clicked. Daniel was the reporter he'd met in New Orleans. Boston spoke as if he'd invited the journalist. That was interesting, and something else Boston hadn't bothered sharing. Daniel's shit-eating grin said he knew he was getting something juicy. That made two of them. Kaz had no idea what was going on.

Daniel spared a quick glance for the building. "This is an odd choice of a meeting place for an interview."

Boston donned his Prince Charming persona. "You'll feel differently in a moment." Boston switched his attention Kaz's way. He motioned for Kaz to join them. Gritting his teeth, Kaz moved to Boston's side and took his hand. Boston beamed. It was a real smile. Not the one he gave everyone else. Kaz's discomfort melted away. "You remember Daniel, right? You met at the charity event in New Orleans."

Kaz nodded and flashed Daniel a quick smile.

Boston transformed once more, becoming the showman. "The moment I make my offer, it'll become public record and old news, so I invited Daniel here to get the scoop, since he's always been kind with his articles in the past."

Every word Boston said made sense but still managed to sound like total bullshit. "Okay," Kaz said, sounding lost but incapable of hiding it. Daniel, on the other hand, looked like he'd won first place in the world's best ass-kisser competition.

Boston kept up the conversation as if Kaz knew exactly what was going on. "As you know, I'm retiring."

Going by Daniel's bug-eyed expression followed up with a shit-eating grin, Kaz gathered he'd gotten the scoop he'd made the trip for.

Boston didn't let it slow him. "Instead of becoming a complete lay about, Kaz and I have decided to open a restaurant." Boston gestured toward the building. "We were checking over the location we've picked out.

Would you like a tour before the realtor gets away?"

At Daniel's over-the-top enthusiastic nod, Boston headed for the door. He stopped when he realized Kaz hadn't budged. "Come on, baby."

Left with no choice, Kaz accepted the hand Boston extended and linked fingers with him. As one, they stepped inside with Daniel on their heels. Kaz listened as Boston painted the reporter a picture of how he envisioned their new place. He could almost see what Boston did by listening to the sound of his voice. Boston was passionate, and it was catching. Kaz wanted everything the man described because he could hear how badly Boston wanted it. Daniel appeared every bit as enamored. With their tour at an end and the announcement of his retirement handled with amazing care, they climbed into the car while Kaz still waded through his haze of shock. He hadn't known Boston had called Daniel in for an exclusive interview. Hell, he also hadn't been one hundred percent sure Boston would ever announce his retirement. Kaz dug around inside his brain, trying to decide how he felt. He wasn't angry per se. It was closer to confused. Sometimes, Boston was like several people living inside one man, and Kaz never knew what he'd do next.

Kaz couldn't stop staring at Boston's profile. It was like he was looking at a stranger. The shock slowly faded away. He couldn't take it any longer. "What the hell was that all about?"

Boston glanced over and winked. "Marketing and deflecting, baby," Boston said, sounding shameless. "I couldn't avoid announcing my retirement forever. This way, I could show Daniel one hand while keeping him looking at the other. No one will question me giving up one dream to pursue another. There will be no speculations about my health. Everyone will be talking about this place. By the time we open, everyone will be clamoring and making the trip to check it out. Daniel is a huge gossip. He'll have every media outlet ready to cover opening day. You can't buy that kind of publicity."

In that moment, Kaz made a huge discovery. Boston was a publicity genius. His mind worked like no one Kaz had met before. He knew exactly how to maneuver people to get the most exposure while keeping his true self hidden. It was no wonder he had money coming out his ass. He was the Liberace of former athletes. It was fucking sexy.

* * *

Liam: *I went by Merge. Jeff said you'd quit.*

Kaz: *Yeah. A while back.*

Liam: *Why didn't you say anything?*

Kaz: *I didn't think you'd approve.*

Liam: *Why wouldn't I approve. You've hated it there for a while now.*

Liam: *Unless you quit to do something terrible.*

Kaz: *Not something terrible, no.*

Liam: *Fuck this. I'm calling and you'd better answer.*

Kaz couldn't lie. He thought about not answering. When Boston demanded he quit working at Merge, he'd done so for multiple reasons. Mostly, because it seemed to be the right thing to do. He loved Boston. Kaz was determined to do right by him. If Boston was uncomfortable with the way Kaz was propositioned by drunk guys every night, then Kaz was done. At the time, he hadn't considered having to justify his decision to anyone down the road, especially not Liam—who hated Boston.

When the phone rang, Kaz gave in. "Hello?"

"You're not whoring yourself or killing people for money, are you?"

An unexpected burst of laughter escaped Kaz. His shoulders relaxed. It was Liam. If anyone would understand, it was him. He realized now, he should've trusted that Liam wouldn't judge. "No. It's nothing like that. Boston and I are opening a restaurant where Momma Dee's used to be."

"You're opening a restaurant? You?" Before Kaz had time to answer, Liam continued, "Well, really, that makes sense. This town needs more choices, and you worked at your parents' place for years, starting as a kid. If anyone can make a go of it, it's you. I've never heard you mention doing anything like before, though."

"It's a new dream."

For a moment, silence rang through the line before Liam responded. "You mean it's Boston's dream."

Kaz rolled his eyes. "Yes and no. It was his idea, but now I'm getting excited. You know me. I've been kind of listless the past few years—with no real direction." Once the floodgates opened, Kaz confessed too much. "After Boston asked me to quit Merge, I've had to start thinking more seriously about what I want. It's not like I can live off Boston for the rest of my life."

"Actually, you could. From what I understand, he has more money than God. Not all from fighting, of course. He's a brilliant investor."

"Gunnar said that?" Kaz asked, incapable of hiding

107

his shock.

"No. Gunnar never talks about Boston. I heard it from Aden. He's the one who always knows all the gossip. But let's get back to Boston asking you to quit. What's up with that?"

"You know what Merge is like. I've got men shoving their numbers in my pocket all night. I'm no cheat, which you also know, but I want to give this a real go with Boston. That means quitting a job that could come between us. I should've done it a long time ago."

"Huh."

"What's that 'huh' about?"

"Nothing," Liam said, sounding thoughtful. "You just seem more involved with Boston than I expected. I thought—maybe—the two of you were just having fun and living life, but no. This is more. I mean, he isn't known for holding down a healthy relationship. Yet, when you talk about him, it's like you're talking about a different person. You sound like..."

Kaz had to know. "I sound like what? A crazy person?"

Liam cleared his throat. It sounded oddly ominous. "No. You sound like you love him."

Kaz considered lying. He couldn't disrespect Boston like that, even if it meant Liam didn't want to remain friends afterward. "I do. You can call me an idiot if you like, but it won't change anything."

"You're not an idiot," Liam said immediately, taking a huge weight off Kaz's shoulders before ruining it. "It's your heart that's stupid." Liam laughed, taking some of the sting from his words. "But, then again, aren't all of our hearts complete dumbasses? Mankind would die out otherwise. We'd become old and bitter, never willing to give any of ourselves to anyone else."

"True."

"Seriously, though," Liam added. "I don't want to see you get your heart broken. You deserve someone who won't hurt you."

"No such guarantee exists in life. You know that."

"I know," Liam said, sounding disheartened. "Don't stop talking to me about things because it's Boston, okay?"

A smile touched Kaz's lips at Liam's words. "Okay."

"Our friendship can't be broken. Remember?"

"I know." There was a tightness in Kaz's chest. He hoped beyond hope that Liam meant those words. No doubt, Gunnar would have something different to say when Liam recapped this conversation. Kaz had a bad feeling he was about to learn what it was like to lose Liam twice in one lifetime.

Liam: *What's the name of your restaurant? I drove by there the other day and there wasn't a sign up yet.*

Kaz: *I don't know. Boston says it's a surprise. God knows, with him, it could end up being anything. We're serving an entire menu of healthy options. Yet Boston also insists the place has a milkshake bar. So, I'm betting the name will be "Don't Judge Me." What's your guess?*

Liam: *Cream me.*

Kaz: **snort* When are you coming by to see the place?*

Liam: *Not sure.*

Kaz: *Let me guess. Gunnar doesn't want you there.*

Liam: *Pretty much. I'm sorry.*

Kaz: *I understand.*

*

Liam: *I was in Miami and stopped at this ice cream joint. They were mixing yummy goodness into each scoop—like candy and whatnot. Is Boston planning on doing something similar?*

Kaz: *Sort of, but it's all going in a blender.*

Liam: *You should name one of the shakes a combination of your names. I'd drink a Boston Kaz-berry shake.*

Kaz: *I think you'd be the only one. LOL!*

*

Kaz: *Mom wants to know if she'll be seeing you at this year's big BBQ.*

Liam: *Will Boston be there?*

Kaz: *I'll tell her no.*

Chapter 7

Boston wasn't wearing a shirt. His jeans weren't buttoned or zipped either. Kaz had already decided the man was also going commando. From his position on the couch, he couldn't miss seeing everything. Several times, Kaz had wiped his palms on his thighs, trying to ignore the hunger growing in his gut. Boston kept pacing from the kitchen to the living room and back again as he thought of new things to add to their ever growing grocery list. Personally, Kaz thought the man enjoyed torturing him with the sight of his delicious body.

By the tenth pass, Kaz broke. After snagging Boston around the waist, he dragged the man between his knees. With his face pressed against Boston's stomach, Kaz sucked in a deep breath. He absorbed the feel of Boston's skin against his. The sensation of Boston's hands caressing his shoulders. Boston's scent tickling his nose.

"You okay?"

For a moment, Kaz couldn't answer. All he could do was hold tight as love swelled in his chest. Six months they'd been living under the same roof. For over a year, they'd been a couple. Half the time, they'd been a secret. All the time, Boston was his reason for breathing.

"Sometimes, I don't want to let go," Kaz finally said, trying to explain what was happening in his head. Boston did something to him. Stole pieces of his soul. Made him say things he knew he would turn over in his head a million times if Boston ever left.

Boston shifted positions, going down onto his knees until they were eye level. "Kiss me," Boston said, sounding every bit as desperate as Kaz felt and soothing his pride.

Moving slowly, Kaz cupped Boston's face and inched closer. He held the man's gaze as he went. They seemed a lighter blue today than usual. By the time their lips met, Kaz's stomach cramped with hunger. Their lips brushed in the softest caress. Barely parted, they lingered. Boston's breath fanned his cheek. It sounded ragged. Neither of them attempted to deepen the kiss. Boston tugged, luring Kaz onto the floor with him. As soon as Kaz had Boston sprawled out on his back, he finally sought Boston's tongue. Their tongues met. Kaz's entire body lit up like a rocket.

"Oh, God," Kaz breathed against Boston's mouth. "What are you doing to me?" He didn't expect an answer. Kaz should've known Boston had one.

"Destroying you for all others, because you're mine."

Damn. It was true. Kaz already knew no one else would measure up. If anything ever happened between them, Kaz would spend the rest of his life comparing everyone to this, and they'd fail. Boston's tongue swiped the roof of Kaz's mouth before retreating.

"So in love with you."

Boston's whispered claim had Kaz on the attack. He stroked and massaged every inch of Boston's body he could reach. For so long, he'd been completely empty. This man had come along and filled every space with light and hope. Instead of focusing on getting through the day, Kaz now spent his time plotting and planning—setting goals for a future filled with all things Boston. Still, he craved more. He wanted to turn over every stone of Boston's life and embed himself there.

His body screamed for him to take Boston right then—enjoy as much of him as he could. Instead, Kaz settled down beside him and linked his fingers through Boston's. He spent a minute staring at him, enjoying the view. Boston's lips were swollen. Kaz wanted to pat himself on the back. He'd done that. The desire for more wouldn't ebb. He needed Boston to feel as exposed as he did. Kaz wanted to know Boston would turn their every conversation over in his head as well.

"What's it like being Boston Tyler?"

An uncomfortable-sounding chuckle escaped Boston. "We live under the same roof. You know me."

Kaz toyed with Boston's fingers while trying to put his thoughts into words. "Yeah, I know you, but I don't know the Boston Tyler whose name pops up on the news and people beg for autographs. I want to hear what that's like for you."

Boston stared at their clasped hands and chewed on his bottom lip. Kaz couldn't look away. Everything about this man called to him. He wanted to memorize every tiny idiosyncrasy.

"It's exhausting," Boston said after a minute.

"How so?"

Rolling onto his back, Boston tugged Kaz along. After settling onto Boston's chest, Kaz tilted his chin up and watched Boston stare at the ceiling. Chill bumps rose on his skin as Boston absently stroked the back of his arm.

"Everyone feels like a ticking time bomb," Boston said, as if his thoughts had finally come together. "All the time, I'm surrounded by people who smile at me.

Sometimes, they're smiling because they like me—in a professional sense. The rest of the time, they're smiling because they're hoping I'll make any misstep at all they can use against me. They can't wait to see me fail. I'm constantly holding my breath, waiting to discover who's who, because they all seem the same on the outside. Unfortunately, the only way I ever find out is when they come at me. Like I said, exhausting."

Boston made fame sound terrible. "I'm surprised you tried building any sort of relationship with me then, or anyone really." As he said the words, Kaz finally understood the bare walls of Boston's old house. Everyone must've felt so fake and pointless.

Boston's arms tightened around him. "You told me once you didn't care about the fame at all when we met. I already knew that. You looked right through me until I forced you to see me. Mostly, you were too busy staring at Liam to see anyone else, but it mattered that you didn't want anything from me."

Kaz felt the need to clear something up since this wasn't the first time Boston had mentioned Liam. "You realize it's always been Liam's friendship I've been desperately clinging on to, right? I mean, for a while, I did want him back, but—mostly—I was scared shitless of losing my best friend."

Boston's fingers froze mid-stroke. He tilted his chin at an angle and met Kaz's gaze. "Now, because of me, you've lost him."

A wave of sadness washed over Kaz, but he couldn't let Boston believe that. "No. If it's anyone's fault, it's Gunnar's. But we're still talking. Everything will work out."

A knock landed on the front door and Kaz's gaze shot to the slab of wood that separated them from the unexpected visitor. Kaz focused on Boston. "You didn't call the press again, did you?"

The sound of Boston's low chuckle against Kaz's ear made him smile. Kaz loved the way it vibrated against his cheek when he was sprawled across Boston's chest like this. With a sigh, Kaz pushed to his feet. Before he reached the door, he glanced over his shoulder, ensuring Boston was sufficiently clothed, since Kaz had done his best to dishevel him. Nothing was hanging out and Boston was on his feet, zipping his jeans. Another knock sounded, louder this time. Kaz answered. For a moment, he stared at Aden, torn between confusion over his presence and worry. Boston might really kill him for all Kaz knew. "Aden," Kaz said for lack of anything more, wondering if this would get ugly.

"Can I speak with you?" Aden's gaze flickered over Kaz's shoulder before adding, "Alone."

Kaz spent a moment debating what he should do—which was the lesser of two evils? He could let Aden insult Boston to his face, since—no doubt—that was what this visit was about, or he could let Aden insult Boston by stepping outside with him. Kaz rubbed the ache blooming between his eyes. He took a step forward, forcing Aden to take one back, and pulled the door closed behind him. Boston never allowed anyone to insult him. Kaz would do the same.

"How have you been?" Aden asked the moment they were alone while eyeing Kaz as if inspecting him for injuries.

"Great. Thanks for asking. And you?" Kaz bit back a laugh at the ridiculousness of their conversation. Surely Aden hadn't wanted to speak with him alone just to ask how he'd been.

"Good. Good," Aden repeated, as if in no hurry to get to the point. "So, he's moved in, has he?"

Since Aden seemed to always know everything and Kaz wasn't ashamed, he didn't deny it. "Yeah, about six months ago."

"Heard he retired."

Kaz shrugged. What could he say? By now,

Boston's retirement was common knowledge.

"Also heard he's opening a restaurant down the road."

Kaz nodded, waiting for the other shoe to drop.

"That's good."

"It is," Kaz said for lack of anything else.

"You'll never know the real Boston," Aden warned, finally coming to his point. Kaz nearly sighed in relief. "Boston has a hundred personalities living inside him. He'll pull out a different one for every situation, ensuring you're always on your toes—never settling into a genuine relationship."

A smile exploded across Kaz's face. Aden had done a damn good job of describing Boston. "Yep. That's him."

Aden gave Kaz a sideways look. "Yet, you're still smiling," Aden said, drawing out every word.

"Of course I am," Kaz said without missing a beat. "Every one of those hundred personalities you described are in love with me."

"That's what Gunnar thought too until he caught Boston in bed with someone else."

"I've heard."

Aden pursed his lips. "You don't seem too concerned. No offense, but you're no better than

119

Gunnar. There's nothing stopping him from doing you the same way."

Kaz shrugged. "You're right. I'm no better or worse than Gunnar. He may very well decide I'm not enough for him one day. The thing is, I can't control that, and it's no reflection on me. I love him, and all I can do is keep loving him while hoping for the best. That's the only factor I can control. Everything else is out of my hands."

Aden shifted from one foot to the other, looking every bit as determined as when their conversation started. It couldn't have been more obvious Kaz had done nothing to change the man's mind. "I can tell you've convinced yourself you can live with losing Boston. Gunnar thought the same."

A sad smile touched Kaz's lips. He shook his head. "That's not true at all. I didn't say a word about being able to live with losing Boston. I said, I can't control it. If he decides I'm not enough for him, it'll rip my heart to shreds, and I'll never be the same. But, you know what? I've been there before and I survived. When I lost Liam, I wanted to die, but I wouldn't have traded a single day we spent together to avoid a hundred years of pain. It's the same with Boston. I wouldn't miss this for anything."

A strained smile touched Aden's lips, and he took a step back. "Well, I see you've already been pulled down the rabbit hole. There's no sense in me trying to talk to you about it." Aden took another step back. He shoved his hands in his pockets, and—out of habit—Kaz's gaze dropped to the man's massive arms. He couldn't say he was unmoved by the way they flexed. Aden was a sexy man. One day, someone would be lucky to snag him. "Don't lose my number, though, okay?" Aden added while still walking backward. He paused next to Boston's car and looked over. "I always did love this car," he said, peering through the driver's side window. "Makes me wonder if I'd stuck with boxing instead of training if I could afford a '71 Hemi Cuda? Huh. It's a four-speed. Nice." He met Kaz's gaze and smiled. "Don't know how I feel about this color, though. I'm not much on blue."

Funny. Kaz loved all things blue, especially Boston's eyes. "I'll be sure to tell Boston how much you hate it."

Aden's smile turned genuine. "I appreciate that. It was good seeing you again."

"You too," Kaz said, unsure if he was lying or not. He liked Aden, but this hadn't been pleasant. Kaz watched Aden climb into his car. He couldn't help but wonder if it he'd be seeing Boston or Liam next with the same lecture. For the sake of their friendship, he hoped not. This was his life now. All he wanted was to be accepted.

*

After finding a shirt, Boston sat down on the couch to wait. He took turns holding his breath and glaring at the door while fuming. As much as he wanted to storm outside and physically throw Aden off their property, Kaz needed to deal with things his way. Boston needed to know how Kaz would deal with things his way. If he could be talked out of their relationship, then they weren't as strong as Boston believed. When the door finally swung open, revealing Kaz, Boston squashed the urge to jump to his feet. Instead, he stayed put on the couch, trying to appear unfazed.

"Was that your intervention?"

"It was," Kaz said as he crossed the room and climbed onto the couch before straddling Boston's hips. The weight of the man he loved in his lap was delicious relief.

"Will you be headed to rehab, then?"

The smile stretching Kaz's lips was sexy as fuck. It had Boston's heart racing. "Are you joking? I'm happy in my addiction."

"You look happy," Boston said, running his fingers up Kaz's spine. He really did look ecstatic. The idea had pride swelling in Boston's chest. He loved this man so fucking hard. It was past time he did everything within his power to hang on to him. "How far would you go to get me on the same level with you?"

"I'd do anything," Kaz said without hesitating and proving he had no sense of self-preservation.

"Good. Get in the car."

The surprise crossing Kaz's features was almost comical. "Why?"

"Because I said so," Boston said, standing and nearly dumping Kaz on his ass in the process. "You said you'd do anything, and I'm calling you on it. Get in the car." Boston headed for the bedroom. Once there, he grabbed his car keys off the dresser and one more item he wouldn't be showing Kaz quite yet. He turned, half-expecting Kaz to be hot on his heels and demanding answers. Instead, Kaz was standing at the front door—waiting.

"Which car are we taking?"

"Mine."

At his answer, Kaz opened the door and stepped out. As always, Kaz's unwavering trust wowed Boston. Anyone else would've dug in their heels and refused to budge until Boston told them what was going on. Kaz was unlike anyone else. He had a way of taking a step back and removing his feelings from every situation—handing his well-being over to Boston with complete abandon. Boston planned to test that today. If, in the end, Kaz chose to back down, Boston would accept his decision. But Boston didn't intend to leave the man much choice.

One of the great things about Key Largo was everything was five to ten minutes away from everything else. It was a small town with light traffic most hours of the day. Kaz made the ride in silence. He didn't ask questions or make small talk. Instead, he toyed with Boston's free hand as he drove. Several times, Boston caught his lips turning up at the edges for no reason at all. He loved this man. Maybe his smile was for every reason in the world. After pulling into the county clerk's office, Boston killed the car and waited. He stared at Kaz's profile while Kaz eyed the building.

"So, my doing anything to make you happy involves getting your car tags?"

"We're not getting car tags. At least, not today."

Kaz looked over. His expression was on lockdown. "Then why are we here?"

Boston tried fighting back his smile as he dug

124

around in his pocket. When he pried out what he'd been looking for, Boston passed the small box over to Kaz as he answered, "We're getting married."

Kaz lips puckered before shifting to one side as if he fought back a thousand retorts as he opened the ring box. He stared down at the matching platinum bands Boston had picked out for them. He licked his lips. "There's a three-day waiting period in Florida."

"Not if one person isn't a resident and my license still shows I live in New Orleans."

Kaz snapped the box closed and opened his car door. "All right then," he said as he climbed from the car.

Boston nearly crowed with laughter. Kaz wasn't shutting him down, but it was equally obvious he'd decided he wouldn't show Boston an ounce of happiness over this, since Boston hadn't asked. Before Kaz made it ten steps toward the door, Boston closed the distance between them and wrapped his arms around Kaz's waist. He hauled the man back against his chest, halting Kaz's steps.

"Surely you didn't picture me getting down on one knee to ask," Boston said against Kaz's ear.

"No," Kaz said before adding, "I pictured I'd get down on one knee and ask, and you'd demand a prenup. Then I'd sign it because I love you and don't want your money."

Boston couldn't decide if Kaz was serious or intended for him to laugh. It wasn't happening. Clasping Kaz's jaw, Boston held Kaz in place as he touched his lips to the shell of Kaz's ear. "Everything I have is yours because it means nothing without you."

Kaz turned his head, meeting Boston's gaze. "Because you're always saying shit like that, I didn't even consider saying no."

"I wouldn't have let you say no."

Kaz smiled. "I know."

As Kaz pulled out of his hold and headed for the door, Boston realized something he never had before—with Kaz, Boston didn't know if he was leading or being led.

* * *

Since the new floors were going in and the painters were coming right after that, Boston and Kaz had a few days to kill before they could get back inside the restaurant to finish up. Boston being Boston, he'd refused to give up until Kaz chose someplace for a short honeymoon. They'd both wanted to go somewhere peaceful and secluded. After tossing several ideas around, they'd chosen a trip to the mountains. Of course, he hadn't considered that it was December and cold as hell the higher you went. Kaz didn't even own a coat. Boston found out the hard way how much Kaz hated being cold. The man hadn't complained, of course. Instead, Kaz shook so hard Boston wondered if he'd shaken any fillings loose. Boston did what he did best—he used this newfound knowledge to his advantage. After firing up the fireplace in their secluded cabin, he'd gathered all the pillows and blankets and tossed them onto the floor in front of the fire. Kaz's gaze followed Boston's every move, but he stayed sitting on his hands and clamping his teeth to keep them from chattering. Boston could feel the man's heated stare lingering on his skin, making Boston burn. It seemed, even freezing to death, Kaz's desire didn't wane. The idea had Boston near to panting. He intentionally dragged his feet, letting the anticipation build.

"Are we building a fort?"

Boston flashed Kaz a smile. "Would you like to?"

Kaz shrugged. "I thought that's where this was headed."

Boston eyed the mound of linens on the floor. "I have to admit I know nothing about building forts. If you want one, I'll try, but my plan was to help you get warm and then fuck you on the floor."

"All right," Kaz said, sounding willing.

Faking exhaustion, Boston collapsed onto the blankets. "I'm done for. You'll have to do all the work."

Kaz didn't move. Boston turned his head. Kaz eyed him with interest. "Give me a reason."

Boston bit back a chuckle as he pretended to misunderstand. "Well, I did build you a fire. Gathered the supplies for a fort, and I'm willing to keep you warm."

"No," Kaz said, sounding turned on. "Strip and give me a reason to join you."

Boston clucked his tongue. "Damn. Marriage changed you. I give you my last name and you repay me with getting all pushy. Good thing I like that in a husband."

"You have much experience with husbands? Don't answer that," Kaz said before Boston had time to respond. Not that he was stupid enough to do any such thing. Kaz pulled his shirt over his head. Boston's mouth went dry. "Your turn, Boston."

Boston did as told.

Kaz unzipped his pants.

Boston did too. That was as far as he went. He didn't set his erection free—the way he wanted.

Instead, he slipped his hand inside his underwear and kneaded his hard cock. "Is this what you want?" he taunted. His hips left the floor, unconsciously seeking the pleasure his palm offered. "Or were you hoping for more?"

"More," Kaz said, his voice thick with lust.

Boston pushed his jeans down his hips, baring his hip bones, but intentionally keeping his erection covered by his underwear. A wet spot formed on the material, giving a hint to how close Boston was to the edge. His stomach gnawed with hunger. Clawing need tore at Boston's skin. When it came to Kaz, Boston was always half a breath away from coming in his jeans. The man did something to him—held some power over Boston's body. It was like he owned Boston's manual and knew how to use all his buttons.

"Show me my toy," Kaz demanded.

Boston couldn't deny him any longer. The cool air mixed with the raging heat of the fire; it brushed over his hardened nipples, only making matters worse. He felt everything times ten—was more aware of his skin. He wiggled out of his clothing.

"Touch yourself," Kaz said, his voice deepening.

Boston couldn't deny him. He palmed his erection. His eyes fell closed as the pleasure tightened the muscles in his stomach.

Kaz's breathing deepened. Boston heard it happen. "Let your knees fall open so I can see that gorgeous ass."

Fuck. Kaz would be the death of him. It was their honeymoon. To his amazement, Boston realized he wanted their first time as a married couple to go down in the history books as the hottest sex ever. At this rate, he'd come without Kaz ever touching him. Still, he let his legs fall open. Kaz finally stood. Boston watched as he stripped out of the remainder of his clothing. He was near to writhing on the floor and begging for Kaz's touch. Instead of joining him, Kaz walked away. Boston watched it happen with a mixture of confusion and curiosity. Relief raced through him when Kaz quickly returned with a bottle of lube.

He tossed it down beside Boston. "I know you like it rough, babe. But I need you to be comfortable for a long ride today. You're not moving from this spot for a while." The promise in Kaz's voice couldn't be missed. Neither could the way Kaz's cock gleamed with moisture as he stroked himself, making Boston realize he'd already lubed up. This time, Boston writhed. His body was out of his control. He needed relief.

"Tell me what you want," Kaz demanded, sounding

fierce.

Reaching between his legs, Boston toyed with his asshole, taunting Kaz as he answered, "Your dick. Right here. Fucking me—hard."

Kaz dropped to his knees between Boston's. "Remember. You asked for it."

That was all the warning Boston got before Kaz pushed his way inside all the way to the hilt. With his ankles draped over Kaz's shoulders, Boston had little control over their pace. Kaz took Boston's ass every bit as rough as Boston liked. Sweat coated Boston's body. His ass stung but felt deliciously full as Kaz hit all the right spots. Boston tugged at his cock, mindlessly seeking relief from the heaviness in his balls and beating at his crown. The sight of Kaz above him, fighting back his orgasm, did something to Boston's chest. He knew this man—his scent, his every expression, and the feel of his body against Boston's as he slept. Boston knew Kaz well enough to know he was about to come, beating Boston to the punch. Realization sank in along with the knowledge of how thoroughly he knew Kaz—Boston couldn't live without him. That had never happened to him before. He'd never encountered a single object or person he couldn't live without, but he'd kill anyone who dared come between them. There'd be no broken heart or licking his wounds; he'd straight up murder someone and then die from the loss of Kaz. This was love. It was also obsession and addiction. This was a madness he'd fully embraced with both eyes open and arms held wide.

Kaz's cried out. The sound stole Boston's orgasm. He shook from the power of the spasms. Kaz's mouth covered his as Boston's cum shot out, filling the space between them. Kaz rocked against him, dragging the ecstasy on. Boston nipped and sucked at Kaz's mouth, trying to consume him. He needed closer. The man's taste was the most amazing flavor on the planet. Boston wanted to sip it all day for the rest of his life.

"This is till death do us part," Boston said, letting his lips brush Kaz's with every syllable.

"Longer than that," Kaz agreed before adding, "No one comes between us."

He'd make them stop trying, Boston silently vowed. If it was the last thing he did, he would force the entire world to love them together, the same as he did.

*

Liam: *Do you want to tell me why you sent me a check for $400?*

Kaz: *It's for your tires.*

132

Liam: *The ones you slashed?*

Kaz: *You knew about that?*

Liam: *Once things settled down, and I had time to think it over, it wasn't hard to figure out.*

Kaz: *You never said anything.*

Liam: *Why would I? Every time it's counted, you've never let me down. When I think about how far I'd go, if I lost Gunnar, tires are nothing. I hope if that day ever comes, you won't judge me, because I plan to do some crazy shit to get him back.*

Kaz: *I'll drive.*

Liam: *And that's why I'm not cashing this check. Love you, babe.*

Kaz: *Love you too.*

Chapter 8

The smell of sweat, old leather, and testosterone filling the air was one of the many reasons Boston hadn't made this trip before now. He'd known the moment that scent permeated his skin, the gnawing desire to be in the ring would fill his gut. He'd been right. His eyes fell closed as he walked through the doors of Aden's training room. The rhythmic sound of gloves hitting bags assailed his senses. Jesus. He missed this more than he could put into words.

Swallowing hard, he opened his eyes and let go of his dream. It didn't take long for his gaze to find Aden. His red hair and massive size made him stand out in any crowd. With his hands on his hips and an evil glare in Boston's direction, Aden stood with his feet braced apart, waiting for Boston to close the distance between them. With an inner sigh, Boston did just that, since he'd put this off too long.

"Never thought I'd see the day you'd show your face around here," Aden said the second Boston was within earshot.

Boston opened his mouth, ready to be a smartass. A young blond guy covered in sweat stepped into

Boston's path. His huge smile had Boston pulling up short of his goal. Worn boxing gloves and a Sharpie filled the man's hands. "Can I get your autograph, Boston?"

Boston didn't hesitate accepting the Sharpie. "Sure. Do you want me to make it out to anyone in particular or just sign?" There were always two sets of people. One liked to have things autographed in their name for bragging rights. The other liked an autograph they could sell. Either way, Boston wasn't bothered. Without fans, he wouldn't have made a dime. He would've kept fighting anyhow, but he couldn't deny he loved the money too.

"If you could make it out to Brian, that would be great."

By the time he finished with Brian's autograph, seven more people had lined up behind the man. Boston intentionally didn't look Aden's way. No doubt the man was fuming. Aden hated for anyone to disturb his tightly run ship. Since aggravating Aden suited his purposes just fine, Boston deliberately dragged his feet, signing as much stuff as possible and conversing with everyone.

It didn't take long for Aden to snap. "Is there a point to this visit? Or are you flexing your star power?" At

Aden's growled question, the men scattered. Boston hid his relief behind a mask of indifference.

"I came to hear your apology."

At Boston's claim, Aden threw his head back and roared with laughter. Several eyes slid their way before quickly returning to their set tasks. Aden swiped at his eyes. "That's a good one. You'll be riding bareback alongside the four horsemen before you hear a breath of apology from me. I like Kaz. Someone needed to be the one to warn him off you."

It wasn't an easy thing, hearing anyone claim liking his husband, especially since he knew Aden didn't mean as a friend. "I'm not talking about Kaz. You said you hated the color of my car. I'll be hearing you grovel over the insult."

Instead of taking it as the joke Boston intended, Aden's face hardened. "I should've known you'd care more about an insult to your car than any man."

"You can't stop being angry for a second. Can you?"

Aden's glare didn't let up. "No."

With his hands clasped behind his back, Boston moved closer. A sigh escaped him at the hatred written on Aden's face. "You're too young to be such a crotchety old bastard. I've never met anyone else who could hold so tightly to a grudge they could turn it into a diamond."

"You hurt my boy," Aden shot back.

"Yes. I did." It wasn't as if Boston could deny it. "But I wasn't alone in that. Was I?"

"I won't train you."

Boston bit back a laugh. The bastard was determined to argue rather than simply ask why Boston was there. "You know I'm retired now. I don't need a trainer."

Aden's face screwed up in confusion. "I'm not looking to hire no one either."

This time, Boston didn't bother pointing out any further facts. Aden was such a stubborn ass. Boston could be too when he set his mind to it. He stared at Aden while chewing the inside of his cheek and waiting.

Aden growled. "Fine. I'll bite. Why are you here?"

"You've done a lot of nipping at my back the past few years," Boston said, pointing out the obvious. "I had to see if it would stand when you're looking me in the face."

To his surprise, Aden's shoulders fell. "What do you want from me, Boston?"

"Stay away from my husband—"

"You're married?" Aden asked, interrupting him.

Boston hardened his voice. He was tired of playing nice. Kaz was the only person who got to have the good side of Boston. Aden should've felt lucky to be dealing with the civil side of him. "Yes. We're married. It's time for you to back away. I've let your shit slide because you're no threat to me, but Kaz is mine. Don't come around again. That is, unless you want Gunnar to know the truth. You know I'm not above telling him everything."

Aden snorted, but Boston didn't miss the hint of fear in Aden's eyes. "He wouldn't believe anything coming from you."

A smirk pulled at Boston's lips. The evil smile was beyond his control. "Doesn't matter. The truth would be out, and the doubt would claw at the back of his brain. If there's anyone who hangs on to things longer and harder than you, it's Gunnar." The sun reflecting off a car as it pulled into the parking lot flashed at the corner of Boston's vision. Turning his head, he caught sight of Gunnar climbing from his truck. Boston's evil smile grew. "Should I wait here and let's find out?"

Aden shot a desperate look toward the parking lot before meeting Boston's gaze once more. "Fine. You twisted bastard. I'll leave Kaz be."

"Good." Boston turned, intent on leaving, since

he'd gotten his way. Aden stopped him before he could get away.

"One of these days, Kaz will see you for the monster you are. What will you do then?"

Because he was the bastard Aden claimed him to be, Boston tossed a wink over his shoulder. "He already knows I'm a monster. Some people prefer a sinner over a saint."

Without waiting for Aden's retort, Boston headed for the door. He held it open for Gunnar as he left. Gunnar met his stare as he passed but gave no hint to his thoughts about Boston being there. Boston dipped his chin in acknowledgment and moved along. Dealing with Gunnar wasn't on his to-do list today.

* * *

Boston was so fucking exhausted. Staying in bed for a week sounded like heaven. If they ever hoped to open, then time wasn't a luxury Boston could afford. Every day, it was getting harder to hide the restaurant's name from Kaz. In all honesty, it wasn't some amazing name, but he'd told Kaz it was a surprise and had so much fun torturing the man with the secret, he'd needed to keep the game going. However, this weekend, the sign was going up on the building. Boston wouldn't be able to keep it under wraps after that. As it was, he was already hiding staff uniforms, menus, and had a shipment of table cards coming he'd have to stash too.

Kaz's hands landed on Boston's shoulders. Boston's eyes fell closed as Kaz massaged his rapidly tightening muscles. He set down the glass he'd been cleaning before he dropped it and gave himself over to Kaz's loving hands. Dropping his chin to his chest, Boston soaked up the sensation of Kaz pressing closer. His lips parted on a pant when Kaz's mouth touched his nape. Kaz had a way of always making life better. It was as if he knew when Boston needed him the most.

"I couldn't take it a second longer," Kaz said against Boston's skin. "You look so damn sexy standing here— working. Sometimes I have to touch you and prove to myself you're real."

"And now that you have?" Even to Boston's ears, he sounded breathless.

Kaz's teeth scraped Boston's neck at the question, causing chill bumps to rise on his skin. "My soul is singing."

"I hope it's singing a rock-n-roll love song, and not country."

Kaz's chest shook with barely suppressed laughter. The low rumble of his chuckles vibrated against Boston's nape.

"Kaz."

"Yeah?" Kaz asked between kisses on Boston's neck.

"Thank you."

Kaz set his chin on Boston's shoulders. "For what?"

"Everything," Boston answered honestly before adding, "Loving me."

"That's the easiest thing I've ever done in my life," Kaz said, sounding sincere. He went back to torturing Boston, kissing his nape and shoulder while skimming his lips lightly across Boston's neck. Kaz startled. Boston felt his slight jump before Kaz pulled his phone out of his back pocket.

"Looks like that package you've been waiting on was delivered. I'll run to the house and pick it up. Do you need anything while I'm gone?"

"Just you to hurry back," Boston answered while still trying to shake off the slight haze coating his vision from Kaz's caress. His brain searched for the memory of which package he'd been expecting. The table cards floated to the surface of his mind. He spun in Kaz's arms. "Don't you dare open that box."

Kaz smile wickedly. "I won't. Cross my heart."

"Why don't I believe you?"

"I have no idea," Kaz said, sounding like a mischievous child.

"If you open that box, I will spank you."

Kaz snorted. "Was that your real threat? If so, I'm totally about to open this damn package."

"Shit," Boston spat, realizing too late his mistake. "Okay. I won't spank you. As a matter of fact, I never will again if you peek."

Kaz donned his best fake frown. "Fine. I'll behave."

Before Boston had time to gloat over his win, Kaz swept in and captured Boston's mouth. By the time Kaz allowed Boston to come up for air, Boston had forgotten what they were talking about. "I'll be back in ten minutes."

"Where are you going?"

Kaz rolled his eyes and headed for the door. Boston refused to admit he was serious. But he did consider calling Kaz back for more than a kiss. That is, until he spotted Gunnar headed for the front door. Kaz held it open for him. The pair spoke briefly in quiet tones before Kaz waved over his shoulder, leaving them alone.

Gunnar's expression gave nothing away. He

could've been there for any reason whatsoever. No matter what, Boston braced himself for an argument. He couldn't think of single civil excuse for Gunnar's presence.

"You're opening a restaurant."

Boston snorted at Gunnar's statement of the obvious and picked up the glass he'd been cleaning before Kaz had started toying with him. "Is your next line 'this town isn't big enough for the two of us'? If so, wow. You should get over yourself."

"Not at all," Gunnar said, snagging a stool on the opposite of the bar, as if he meant to stay a while and surprising Boston. He sat and eyed Boston. "I'm here to talk about Liam and Kaz. The two of them have been friends a long time. They should get to stay that way."

"Nobody is stopping them."

Gunnar's mouth flattened into a hard line. "Actually, I sort of am."

That revelation didn't surprise Boston. On the other hand... "Never thought I'd hear you admit to a single wrongdoing."

"I'm not so sure I am wrong," Gunnar shot back. "You're not a good person, Boston. You never have been. I'm not certain you have it in you."

The smile stretching Boston's lips was out of his

control. "You're doing a lot of pointing out the obvious today."

"The thing is," Gunnar said, as if Boston hadn't spoken. "Even though I know you're the biggest piece of shit that ever walked the planet, I also think you really do love Kaz. Possibly, he's the first person you've ever loved other than yourself."

Boston clamped his back teeth together with enough pressure to crack a tooth. Gunnar had earned an insult or two, but Boston would only stand so much bullshit from the man.

"Yet you had him quit his job. What kind of shit is that?"

"Sounds to me like Liam and Kaz are still talking," Boston said, more for himself than Gunnar. There was no way Gunnar would've known Boston asked Kaz to quit, unless Kaz had told Liam. He wiped off another glass and shoved it in the cabinet underneath the bar before tackling Gunnar's question. "Liam quit his job for you. Why is it any different for Kaz? Should he have stayed at a job he hated because you don't like how I convinced him to quit?"

"Liam didn't quit his job immediately, and he didn't do it because I demanded it," Gunnar answered, sounding pissed off.

"I've been with Kaz for well over a year now. He didn't quit immediately either," Boston shot back, nonplussed. He didn't bother checking Gunnar's reaction over that confession. "Kaz hated that job. I knew it, so I found a way to save his pride and let him walk away from it."

"You've been together for over a year?"

At the accusation in Gunnar's voice, Boston released a heavy sigh, set his elbows on the bar, and focused on Gunnar. "What are you digging for, Gunnar?"

Gunnar ran his hand through his hair, leaving it standing on end. Boston had always found that move sexy on Gunnar, but as he stared at the man now, he felt nothing. Kaz owned Boston. All the way to his soul.

Gunnar's eyes sharpened, and he squared his shoulders as if expecting anything. "Do you really love him or is this some game?"

A huge part of Boston wanted to toss a few hateful and well-placed words at Gunnar. He'd love to say something awful and make Gunnar hate him even more than he already did. But Boston did love Kaz, and even his evil streak couldn't deny it. "Not that it's any of your concern, but yes, I love him. Have you ever seen me uproot my life for anyone else? Before Kaz, I would've laughed my ass off at any man who gave up everything simply to be with someone else. Kaz is different."

"Whoa," Gunnar breathed, making Boston want to put his fist in the center of his face. "I never would've believed those words came from you if I hadn't heard them with my own ears. You almost sounded human right then."

Anger rushed through him. Boston's lips tingled. A pain rushed through his jaw as a wave of exhaustion washed over him. "Fuck." The curse fell from Boston's lips as the world went dark.

When Boston opened his eyes, everything was black. In an odd way. Boston blinked. The black surface inches from his face didn't disappear. It was right there and looked soft. He touched it. He was ashamed to admit it took running the tips of his fingers over the surface for his mind to clear enough for him to realize it was a shirt. His head was in a hard lap. His gaze moved upward, meeting gorgeous jade eyes. They were filled with concern. Reaching up, he tried smoothing away the line between Kaz's brows.

"Are you okay?"

Boston licked his lips before answering. He was so fucking thirsty. "Of course. I have you."

"I called the doctor. They're going to move your next appointment up to tomorrow."

He tried nodding, but his head hurt too much. "That's fine."

"What the fuck is going on, Boston?"

An inner groan rang through Boston's mind at the sound of Gunnar's voice. The clearer his mind became, the more that came back to him. He'd been talking to Gunnar when he'd had another episode. Fuck. Boston squeezed his eyes shut. He didn't want this.

Kaz's fingers ran through Boston's hair, soothing him. "Thank God Gunnar was here, and I was only five minutes away."

"Help me up," Boston whispered, hoping the humiliation would pass quickly and he didn't puke on anyone.

Two sets of hands pulled him to his feet. Only his current weakened state kept Boston from jerking from Gunnar's hold. Instead, he braced his palms on the edge of the bar and kept his gaze locked on his hands.

"How long has this been going on?"

The barely suppressed rage in Gunnar's tone had Boston biting back a thousand ugly retorts. "Long enough," he said instead.

"Since before or after the title fight?"

Boston slowly turned his face away from Gunnar, hoping the room would stop spinning. He focused on Kaz. "Help me to the car, baby."

Gunnar let out an impressive litany of curse words before shouldering his way beneath Boston's arm and helping Kaz walk him to the car. "This conversation isn't over," Gunnar said, bitching all the way to the car and doing nothing to help Boston's headache. "If this shit's been happening since before our match, it wasn't a fair fight, and I don't deserve to have the title."

"Gunnar, shut the fuck up," Boston spat through clenched teeth. "Not everything is about you." To Boston's surprise, Gunnar fell silent. His jaw ticked as he lowered Boston into the passenger seat of Kaz's car, but he didn't say another word. Once Kaz shut the door, leaving Boston to the silence of being alone inside the car, Boston reclined the seat and closed his eyes. Goddamn Gunnar. Why had he shown up? He could hear Kaz and Gunnar talking, but it was like a distant rumble of voices. No words would penetrate his fogged brain. This was different from his other seizures. He didn't feel right. Maybe he needed a nap. He heard Kaz say his name, but his eyelids refused to budge. Yep. He needed some sleep.

Chapter 9

You're lucky it isn't CTBI. That would eventually kill him. Epilepsy is treatable. The doctor's words kept racing through Kaz's head as he watched Boston sleep. Thank God Boston had stopped boxing when he had. If he'd kept pushing, he might already be dead. An increase in medication and lower stress was a treatment plan Kaz could live with. He couldn't live with Boston dying or slowly losing himself. When he'd gotten in the car and hadn't been able to wake Boston, Kaz had caught a glimpse of a nightmare—one where he lost Boston forever. He'd never driven to the hospital so fast in his life. It had been hours and still Boston hadn't stirred. Gunnar had left two hours earlier to pick up Liam, leaving Kaz alone with a thousand horrible thoughts. Logically, he knew Boston was only sleeping. His body was worn out and needed rest. Kaz's panicked brain played tricks on him. What if Boston never woke up? What would Kaz do without him? He was terrified.

"I'd really hoped to wake up in our bed with your ass pressing against my crotch."

Kaz's eyes snapped from where he'd been watching

the nurse change out Boston's IV to Boston's face. His eyes were still closed.

"Thanks for that, but I've still got six hours left in my shift," the elderly nurse said, stealing a laugh from Kaz and forcing Boston's eyes open.

A smile stretched Boston's lips. The one that always stole Kaz's breath. "It's just as well. You'd probably break my heart."

"You know it, darling," she said, giving Boston's knee a pat before leaving them alone. Kaz couldn't look away from his husband's gorgeous face. Relief poured through his veins, making him useless.

"I'm sorry."

At Boston's apology, Kaz fought to find his voice. When he did, it came out sounding as if he'd been chewing on glass. "For what?"

"You're wearing your worry line between your eyes again. I promised myself I would make you happy. All I do is scare you."

Kaz tried forcing his face to relax. "You're worth it," Kaz said, coming to his feet and closing the distance between them. "Life with you is never boring," Kaz added as he linked his fingers through Boston's and brought the man's hand to his lips. "How do you feel?"

Boston didn't hide from him. His miserable

expression said it all. "Like I want to go home. I want to crawl into our bed and cuddle. Nothing fixes me the way you do."

"I promise I'll baby the fuck out of you when we get home. First, I need you to work this out, so we don't have to come back." Kaz tightened his hold on Boston's hand. "I need you—period. You can't leave me. Okay?" Kaz didn't mean to bare so much of his soul, but the horror of not being able to wake Boston hadn't dissipated.

Boston toyed with Kaz's hand, seeming lost in thought. When he met Kaz's gaze again, Kaz swore he'd never seen Boston more clearly. "Before you, I was miserable. I hated myself and honestly didn't care if I died in the ring." It was like getting punched in the gut, but Boston wasn't finished. "Then I stayed that first weekend with you, and I couldn't wait to come back for the next. I have so many frequent flyer miles built up we could travel the world," Boston said with a chuckle before his expression turned serious once more. "Every time I left, it was like ripping off my skin. The second I set eyes on you again, it was always like coming home. I was just waiting on you to agree to keep me. So, no. I won't let anything take me away."

He had Boston's word. That was all Kaz needed.

The relief written on Kaz's face had Boston swallowing a lump in his throat. Kaz believed in him with everything he had. There was no greater feeling. Boston tugged, intent on urging Kaz into bed with him. The door opened. Gunnar and Liam poured through. Disappointment hit Boston. Looked like he wouldn't get to hold his husband after all. He hated hospitals. People didn't believe in letting anyone rest.

Liam filled the seat Kaz had vacated moments earlier. Boston dipped his chin in the man's direction. It had been a long time since he'd set eyes on Liam. He knew he still spoke to Kaz, but Gunnar hadn't let the man come around. It was almost funny. There'd always been a hint of jealousy living inside Boston when it came to Liam. Looking at him now, he felt nothing beyond the gratefulness over him supporting Kaz.

No sooner than Liam got settled, Gunnar spoke up. "Can I talk to Boston alone?"

At Gunnar's growled demand, Liam and Kaz exchanged glances. Boston could practically hear their silent conversation. His man was worried and Liam was reassuring him. Liam stood, and with a final glance his way, Kaz let Liam drag him from the room. The moment they were alone, Gunnar jumped in with both feet.

"You've known about this a long time, and you still fucking fought me for the title. That's bullshit, Boston. What if you'd died? Was ruining my life once not enough for you? I would've spent the rest of my life knowing I was the person who'd killed you. That's some real bullshit," he repeated as if he couldn't say it enough.

Boston released a loud sigh. Gunnar never let anything go. It didn't matter that he hadn't died during their match—only that he could have done so. "As I've told you many times in the past, not everything is all about you," Boston said, tired of having to say it. "I don't tell you that to be a dick. Well, not always. Mostly, it's because you don't hear what I'm saying to you. I'm trying to get you to take a step back and look at the big picture." Boston shifted positions in the bed, trying to relieve some of the pressure on his aching back. He didn't know how to talk to people, especially Gunnar. Kaz was the only person who heard what Boston was trying to say—rather than what left his lips. "What happened between us, it wasn't about you. It was about me." Boston tapped his chest, trying to get his point across. "You should've let it go right away. Moved on with your life. I wasn't worth you wasting your fury. You take on concerns that aren't yours. Stop doing that. You can't control anything, especially things that have nothing to do with you. If you think—for some dumbass reason—you don't deserve that title because of my health, then challenge someone else and win. Simple. Problem solved. As far as where we find ourselves now, Kaz doesn't need you to save him. Liam doesn't need you to tell him who to be friends with. I don't need you to tell me I shouldn't have fought you for the title. I'm a grown man who makes his own decisions with no thought to how it impacts you."

He held Gunnar's gaze like he hadn't done in years, trying to make the man see his earnestness. "I love Kaz. If you think your relationship with Liam can somehow be hurt by him remaining friends with Kaz because I exist, then you need to say that back to yourself to see how dumb as shit it sounds. I feel like a real jackass for having said it aloud. Shit just worked out the way it worked out. I don't know why. Maybe there really is some higher power, and he's laughing his ass off right now. For whatever reason, we weren't meant to be, but I was meant to meet Kaz. Just as you were meant to meet Liam. You have to let shit go and just be happy."

"I am happy."

"Then let shit go," Boston shot back at Gunnar's claim. "Yes. I've known for a long minute about the epilepsy. Six months before we split when I fought Steele Fletcher I took a shot to the head."

"I remember."

Boston dipped his chin. "It was one too many. I started having trouble seeing, so the next time you went out of town, I had some tests done. They said I had sustained a brain injury at some point. At the time, they didn't know what the long-term effects would be, but they knew I couldn't continuing fighting."

Gunnar sat down.

"I didn't have my first seizure until three months later while you were in Vegas for a match. See? I won the title, knowing I shouldn't fight. What does losing it—while knowing I shouldn't compete—matter?"

Gunnar looked as if he didn't know whether he should be furious or pitying Boston. "Does anything matter to you at all? Seriously, man. I knew the title meant everything to you, but seriously."

Loving Kaz had changed something inside Boston. His whole life, he'd been taught that a man was only as strong as he could hit. Yet Kaz was strong because he could take one without wavering. That lesson gave him the courage to say things to Gunnar he might not have confessed otherwise.

"I didn't know how to be weak with you," Boston said. Every word came out as if dragged out by an invisible force. "When we were together, you always made me feel powerful, but I never felt like you'd still love me if I couldn't be strong any longer. Not because you did anything wrong. We both know that isn't the case. I didn't..." Boston's hands lifted for a second before falling back to his lap. He didn't know how to explain his feelings. There'd been something fundamental missing between them. Boston hadn't noticed it until he'd needed whatever they were lacking.

"It's okay," Gunnar said, setting him free. "You don't have to explain. I get it. If roles had been reversed, I don't think I would've felt like I could count on you either. We were only good together when we were at our best."

Exactly. They hadn't been meant to weather the lows. "For what it's worth, I'm sorry, and I didn't come here to fuck up your marriage."

Gunnar held his gaze—like a friend. The backs of Boston's eyes burned. It was the first glimpse of the old Gunnar he'd seen in years. They had been friends

157

once.

"I know. You love Kaz. He's a good guy. I'm glad you found someone who'll let you be weak."

A sardonic smile pulled at the corners of Boston's mouth. "Me too, because I'm fucking tired." Boston blew out a breath. "Really fucking tired."

*

"What do you think they're saying in there?"

Liam shook his head. "I don't know, but they need to hash things out."

"Yeah." It was true. In spite of everything they'd been through over the years, Liam was his friend. That friendship had never wavered. Now their men needed to work things out.

"So," Liam said, dragging out the word. "You and Boston. How did that happen? You've never said."

A smile pulled at the corners of Kaz's mouth. Liam was such a great person. He should've known Liam would do his best to accept any decision Kaz made. Kaz leaned his shoulder against the wall and focused on Liam. The man's dark-brown hair, sexy green eyes, and gorgeous body did nothing for Kaz for the first time in his life. Boston was everything now. The knowledge loosened Kaz's tongue.

"Hmmm, well, you know how he showed up to

apologize to you?"

Liam nodded.

Kaz turned inward as half his brain locked on the memory of that day. "He stuck around after you left with Gunnar. For the first time in a long time, I didn't feel quite so alone or hurt as much as usual. Then he showed up a second time and took away a little more pain. Before I knew it, I was smiling again." A small smile tugged at Kaz's lips. "One day, I realized I missed him between visits." Kaz shook his head. Even he couldn't believe the confessions leaving his lips. "I tried fighting it. God knows I didn't want to care about Boston, but it was too late." Kaz forced himself to focus and held Liam's gaze. "He's amazing. I know you probably don't believe that, but he is. He helps my mom cook sometimes and flirts with old ladies to make them smile."

"Looks like he makes you smile too."

Kaz's cheeks ached from it. "Yes. I don't know how to explain it. It's like there's this crazy wonderful person living behind the asshole mask he shows the world, and I'm one of the few people who gets to see the real him—like I'm unique to him," Kaz said, admitting something he'd never confessed to anyone. "Like I'm irreplaceable. Worth redemption."

159

"You're right," Liam said with a sweet smile. "He is amazing. Anyone who can make you happy, exactly as you deserve, has my vote. Doesn't matter who it is. Now, that doesn't mean I won't hate him and get a voodoo doll in his likeness if he hurts you," Liam added.

Kaz snorted. "Of course. You're my best friend. At the very least, I expect a voodoo ritual if I get my heart broken." For a moment, they stared at each other, wearing matching evil grins. They couldn't be broken. "I love you."

Liam didn't hesitate. "I love you too."

Kaz nodded toward the door separating them from Boston and Gunnar. "Should we check on them?"

"Definitely," Liam said, sounding as if he half expected they were killing each other inside.

As one, they burst into the room. Boston's eyes were closed and Gunnar was watching football.

"What the fuck?" Liam said, stealing Kaz's line. "Did you plan to leave us in the hall all day?"

Without opening his eyes, Boston answered, "We figured y'all were exchanging I love yous and all that good shit, so we gave you a minute."

It was a little scary how well Boston knew him. Kaz crossed the room and pulled the string behind

Boston's bed, cutting off the light directly over his head. One of Boston's eyes popped open, and he sighed in relief.

"Thank you. That light was killing my head."

"I know," Kaz said as he lowered the rail on one side of Boston. Boston moved over, making room for Kaz to climb into the tiny bed with him. No sooner than he settled down with his head on Boston's chest, the door opened and the doctor stepped in.

After casting a quick glance around at the room's occupants and dismissing them, the middle-aged man straightened his glasses and focused on Boston. "So far, all of your tests look good. How are you feeling?"

"My head hurts, but otherwise, I'm solid."

The doctor nodded. "I can order you something for the pain."

Boston waved off his offer. "No thanks. Got everything I need right here." Boston's arms tightened around Kaz as he made the claim, making Kaz's heart sing.

Proving the doctor was every bit as kind as he looked, he smiled. "I see that you do. We're going to keep you overnight and make sure this new increase in medicine isn't too much. If you do okay through the night, we'll let you go home in the morning. Home. Not back to working on your new business. Home. To bed."

"Yes, sir," Boston said with a chuckle that vibrated against Kaz's ear.

"What if the medicine isn't working out?" Kaz asked, since it was obvious Boston didn't intend to ask anything at all.

"Then we'll try a different one," the doctor answered without missing a beat. "Don't worry, Mr. Tyler. We still have several options available to us. Your husband isn't going anywhere for a long time." Liam and Gunnar both turned Kaz's way at the doctor's statement. He could feel their accusing gazes upon him. "I'll leave you alone for a little while and let you get some rest. Although it's fine for you to have visitors, I would recommend they don't stay too long. That doesn't count for your husband, of course. I'll have a nurse bring you some extra blankets and pillows, since I assume you're staying the night too."

Kaz nodded. "Thank you." It was too late for Kaz to beg the man to stop calling him Boston's husband. It couldn't have been more obvious that Liam and Gunnar got it. They were married. He hadn't said anything. Not because he was ashamed. He'd never been less ashamed or happier about a single fucking thing in his life, but it was Liam and Gunnar.

The second the door closed behind the doctor, leaving them alone, Liam pounced. "You got married?"

"Yes," Kaz said, sounding proud even to his ears.

Liam shoulders fell. "You didn't invite me." Too late, he realized Liam wasn't upset for the reason Kaz expected.

Like he always did, Boston spoke up, saving Kaz. "That's my fault. I didn't give him time to do anything. It was a surprise. I swept him out the door and married him before he had time to think too much about it and come to his senses."

Kaz pinched his side. "Shut up."

Boston laughed. "Seriously. We might do some sort of reception or whatever later, but with my health and the restaurant..."

"No. You need to be relaxing," Liam argued. He tilted his head to the side and eyed them for a moment. A bright smile lit his face. "You look so happy together."

"Speaking of the restaurant," Gunnar said, coming to his feet. "I told Boston we'd go by and finish unpacking and setting up the last of their stuff."

Kaz's eyebrows hit his hairline at the comment. "Seriously?"

Boston's fingers combed through Kaz's hair. His voice rumbled in his chest and vibrated against his ear when Boston responded, "Yeah. I gave him my keys to the building. Thanks again for offering to help. Normally, I wouldn't accept, but I think I've scared Kaz enough lately."

Liam looked every bit as surprised as Kaz felt, but he still stood and followed his husband to the door. His gaze slid Kaz's way, and a smile lit his face. "It's the least we can do for our friends."

Gunnar grunted but didn't correct him. At the sound, a smile exploded across Kaz's face. They were on their way to healing. One day soon, Boston would sneak his way inside the pair's life. Kaz's respect for Gunnar skyrocketed as he nodded their way.

"We'll get everything fixed up for you. You just get better. Kaz needs you around."

"Thank you," Kaz mouthed, incapable of making his voice work. Until that moment, he hadn't realized how deeply he'd felt the loss of Liam's constant friendship. Seeing it rising again in the distance stole all of Kaz's words.

Chapter 10

"You named the place 'Slip.'"

Boston nodded, looking proud as they stood outside the restaurant hand in hand, staring at their new sign. "It's a boxing term for a defense move—one you make when you're trying to avoid taking a hit. You know, the move I forgot to make," Boston finished with a laugh.

Exasperation rose in Kaz's chest. "That's so not funny, Boston."

Glancing over, Boston eyed Kaz for a moment, looking confused. His brow cleared, and he pulled Kaz into his arms. The instant Kaz found himself engulfed in Boston's embrace, he forgot to care the man he loved had named their restaurant after a boxing maneuver that could've kept him from getting hurt.

Boston pressed his lips to Kaz's cheek in a loud, smacking kiss. "I think you misunderstood, babe. I named our restaurant after the move I forgot to make when I met you. You blew me away. I forgot to guard my heart, and you stole it."

Kaz sniffed loudly, noisily showing he'd been

mollified. "Okay, that I can accept." He held tighter to Boston as the excitement grew. "Tomorrow is the big day. We open our doors and your second biggest dream comes true."

Instead of joining him in celebration, Boston scoffed. "This isn't my second biggest dream. That came true when I married you. This is more like fourth or fifth in line for things I want out of life."

It seemed Boston was on a roll today with the smooth talk. For each second in life Kaz had ever felt alone, unloved, and unwanted, Boston had triple the healing power. As much as Kaz would've loved to bask in the glow of Boston's love, he also really wanted to know what else Boston craved from life.

"What's your third dream?"

If Kaz hadn't been staring at Boston, he might've missed the man's blush. For a full minute, Kaz was speechless. He never would've believed Boston capable of embarrassment. Now, he had to know.

"Don't hold back now," Kaz begged. "Say the words and if I can make it come true, I will."

Boston cleared his throat and shuffled his feet before answering, "I'd like to hang some pictures on the wall."

It was such a simple request. The backs of Kaz's

166

eyes burned. Boston wanted something most people took for granted—memories with people who loved him. Kaz swallowed, trying to fight the stinging sensation.

"Let's start now," Kaz said, pulling his cell phone from his pocket. "Time for a selfie with our new restaurant." After squeezing in close, Kaz held the phone at arm's length. As he snapped the picture, Boston turned his head and pressed his lips to Kaz's cheek. The smile stretching his lips had his cheeks aching as he checked to make sure the picture wasn't blurry. It was perfect. They looked happy and he could make out a hint of the restaurant's sign behind them. He loved it.

"That's awesome," Boston breathed against his ear. "It'll look great on the wall next to pictures of our kids."

"Kids?" Kaz asked, almost dropping the phone in his surprise. He juggled the device from hand to hand until he had it secured. Boston howled with laughter at Kaz's reaction. Kaz opened his mouth, intent on questioning Boston over these new plans. An image of Boston holding a baby flashed through Kaz's mind and the words died on his lips. A wave of longing so intense it nearly blasted Kaz from his feet overcame him. He could see it. This was the life he never expected to want. "Let's do it."

Boston's smile melted away as he realized Kaz was serious. In two strides, Boston closed the distance between them. His mouth came down on Kaz's with enough force their teeth bumped. It was a kiss filled with promise. They were each other's new beginning. It had been that way from the first time they kissed. Maybe they'd started out as a weekend escape, but even when Kaz hadn't wanted to admit it, he'd known they were meant to be. So they'd hang pictures on the wall. It was Kaz's third or fourth biggest dream come true.

Keep an eye out for the next book in the Low Blow series, *Brawler*.

Author Bio

Charity Parkerson is an award winning and multi-published author with several companies. Born with no filter from her brain to her mouth, she decided to take this odd quirk and insert it in her characters.

*2015 Readers' Favorite Award Winner
*Winner of 2, 2014 Readers' Favorite Awards
*2015 Passionate Plume Award Finalist
*2013 Readers' Favorite Award Winner
*2013 Reviewers' Choice Award Winner
*2012 ARRA Finalist for Favorite Paranormal Romance
*Five-time winner of The Mistress of the Darkpath

Connect with her online:

--Website: charityparkerson.com
--Facebook: facebook.com/authorCharityParkerson
facebook.com/TheMenofSin
--Twitter: twitter.com/CharityParkerso

www.ingramcontent.com/pod-product-compliance
Lightning Source LLC
Chambersburg PA
CBHW060225180626
46813CB00007B/2963